A Garland Series

The
Flowering of the Novel

Representative Mid-Eighteenth
Century Fiction
1740-1775

A Collection of 121 Titles

Abdeker

Or, the Art of Preserving Beauty

A. Le Camus

Garland Publishing, Inc., New York & London

1974

Bibliographical note:

this facsimile has been made from a copy in the
Library of the University of Illinois
(x6467.L494aE)

Library of Congress Cataloging in Publication Data

Le Camus, Antoine, 1722-1772.
　　Abdeker; or, The art of preserving beauty.

　　(The Flowering of the novel)
　　Reprint of the 1754 ed., printed for A. Millar,
London.
　　I.　Title.　II.　Series.
PZ3.L4942Ab5　[PQ1993.L79]　843'.5　　　74-17402
ISBN 0-8240-1140-6

Printed in the United States of America

A B D E K E R:

O R,

The Art of preserving

B E A U T Y.

Tranſlated from an Arabic Manuſcript.

L O N D O N,

Printed for A. Millar, in the *Strand.*
M DCC LIV.

*The following ancient Inscription was found on
a Table of Brass, at the Foot of the Serpen-
tine Column in the Hipprodome at* Conftantinople.

ÆSCULAPIUS to PSHYCHE.

NAture had given thee Beauty like unto the
Morning-rofe, but was going to reap thee in
thy Bloom. I have prevented her Strokes: and
the *Serquis* * (which I have given thee) filtred in
thy Veins, has fixed in thee all the ineftimable
Treafures of Youth. *Cupid* could not withftand
thy Charms. He became thy Conqueft, and ren-
dered thee immortal. O divine Art of Phyfic! to
which *Pfhyche* is indebted for Beauty, Love, and
Immortality.

* See the fecond Obfervation.

Place this before the Preface.

THE

PREFACE.

*T*HE *following is a Translation of an* Arabian *Manuscript, which* Diamantes Utasto, *Physician to the* Turkish *Ambassador, brought to* Paris *in the Year* 1740. *The Author of it is well known among the Learned Writers of the present Age.*

This Work is not to be rank'd among the trifling Performances that are daily publish'd, and that have scarce any thing to recommend them but their Novelty, though perhaps at the same time they contain nothing that is new. The Contents of it are agreeable to the Name we have given it. The Author's Design was not merely to amuse the Fair Sex; he has endeavour'd to be useful to them; and his Book deserves to be consider'd as a compleat Treatise of BEAUTY: *For he*

has

*has described at large every thing that can
destroy, preserve, increase, or diminish it;
and he has omitted nothing that has a Relation to its physical or moral Causes. The
Plan of it is altogether singular, and will
doubtless excite the Curiosity of its Readers.
ABDEKER was a Physician; he was in
Love with the most beautiful Lady in the
World; he let her into all the Mysteries of
Beauty, and after so engaging a Manner,
that by reading his Book you will be instructed in all the Secrets of his Art, though you
will be at the same time persuaded that you
have read nothing but the History of his
Amours.*

*It is to be hoped that the Ladies, for whom
this Work is chiefly composed, will not be
much at a stand by the few Terms of Art they
will meet with in reading it. They are so
learned and so accomplish'd now-a-days, that
we cannot, without affronting them, doubt of
their Capacity. I have assisted at some Con-
versations at the Toilet, that were as serious
as most of our Academical Conferences. There
you might hear the Geometrician, the Philosopher, the Divine, the Fop, each speak in
the Language of his Profession. From whence
I infer,*

I infer, that the Dictionary of Physicians is not more contrary to their Taste than the Dialect of Geometricians or Philosophers. In fine, they will find that this little Book was very much wanting to their Library; and since Nature has been pleased to bestow on them the Gift of Beauty, they cannot expect from a Physician a more agreeable Present than the Art of preserving it.

ABDEKER:

A B D E K E R:

O R,

The ART of preserving

B E A U T Y.

PART I.

CHAPTER I.

*A*BDEKER was born at *Mocha* *, where his Parents distinguish'd themselves by their superior Skill in the divine Art of MEDI- CINE. He followed the Profession of his Forefa- thers, for which he had a great Liking; and enjoy'd a very high Reputation in his own Country, a thing easier acquired than preserved: But, in order to im-

A famous City in *Arabia Felix.*

B

prove himfelf, he undertook a Voyage to *Turky*; and
being arrived at *Conflantinople*, refolved to ftay there
for fome time, to converfe with the Phyficians of
that City, who were then accounted the moft learned
in all the Eaft, and who could not deny him the Ap-
plaufe his vaft Genius deferved. The fuperior Talents of this young Foreigner foon became the Wonder and Admiration of the whole City. His great
Succefs made him known both far and near; and
the *Dervifes* cried out, that their great Prophet look'd
upon the *Mufulmans* with a favourable Eye, fince he
had been pleafed to fend them one of his moft faithful Servants, to put a happy End to all their Mi-
fery.

It happened that the Sultan, who reign'd at this
Time *, became dangeroufly ill of a malignant Fever. Death furrounded him on all Sides, and threat-
en'd every Moment to give him the fatal Stroke.
The Doctors, frighten'd at the Approach of the
ghaftly Meffenger, quitted the Sultan's Apartment;
and, as they had nothing in their Power that was
capable of making any Oppofition againft the Prefence of fo formidable an Enemy, refolved to retire.
When they were all gone, *Abdeker* was introduced to
the Sultan: He approach'd him, examin'd his Situation, felt his Pulfe, and immediately, with a Countenance as undaunted as if he had been the Law-
giver of Nature, order'd *Mahomet* to fwallow a Dofe

---

* *Mahomet* the Second, firnamed by the *Turks* Bojuc, that
is, The Great, was born at *Adrianople* on the 24th of *March*,
1430. He fucceeded his Father, who was called *Amurat* the
Second, in the Year 1451.

of

of White Powder *; which produced such happy Effects, that his violent Agitation was soon changed into a perfect Calm. The Fever disappear'd, and *Mahomet*'s Life was prolonged.

THE Sultan, transported with Joy, and penetrated with the most lively Sentiments of Acknowledgment, embraced his Doctor, call'd him his Deliverer, and assured him by the most convincing Expressions, that he should never forget the great Obligation he owed him for prolonging his Life. From this Time *Mahomet* treated *Abdeker* as his intimate Friend, and fear'd nothing more than to lose him: He used all Means to engage him to stay with him; he preferred him to the Office of First Physician, and even did him the Honour to entrust to his Care the Women of the Seraglio, without depriving him of the Members that might excite the Jealousy of a *Turk*; and he order'd his Eunuchs to obey the Doctor in every thing, as they would obey himself. *Abdeker*, after returning him Thanks for all these Favours, went immediately to pay his Compliments to *Irene* the Sultaness, his declared Favourite. Afterwards he was convey'd to the Apartment of the Odalikes: It was there he met *Fatima*; he was forthwith seized by this Lady's Charms, and this was the first Time his Heart became sensible of the Power of Love.

---

* It is to be presumed that this White Powder, which produced so speedy an Effect, was nothing else but the Emetick, that was unknown before this Time to all other Doctors. It is probable that *Paracelsus* might have learnt its Composition from some of those to whom *Abdeker* communicated his Secret.

CHAP.

C H A P. II.

A Defcription of BEAUTY.

FATIMA was bought in *Georgia*. This Coun
try produces the handfomeft Women in the
World; and thither the Eunuchs of the Grand Signior go, to chufe beautiful Women for the Seraglio.
Fatima, at her very firft Entrance, fo much out-fhone
all her Rivals in Beauty, that there was none of them
fit to difpute it with her. *Irene* was the only Perfon
that came neareft to her, but could do nothing to her
Prejudice, for *Mahomet*'s Heart was inflamed and
quite overpower'd by the Love of *Fatima* as foon as
ever he beheld her. It was no Wonder; for her
Charms were fuch, that it was impoffible to fee her
without falling in love with her.

HER Face form'd a perfect Oval; her Eyes were
blue, and full of fweet and pleafing Smiles; her Eye-
brows were brown, and reprefented two correfpond-
ing Segments of two equal Circles. The Height
and Breadth of her Forehead were in due Proportion.
Such Symmetry appeared in the Formation of all
the Parts of her Head, and fuch Majefty fhone in
her Looks, that Nature feem'd to have formed her
Brow to grace an Imperial Diadem. Her Nofe,
which fprung infenfibly from her Forehead, fepa-
rated her rofy Cheeks; her Mouth was fmall and
well form'd; her Vermilion Lips were border'd with
two Rows of Teeth, that reprefented fo many Pearls;
and the loweft Part of her Face was adorn'd by a
Chin

Chin that form'd a perfect Arch. The Face is the chief Seat of Beauty: It there displays all its Force and all its Majesty; it is there it places those powerful Charms that command and captivate the Spectator's Heart, and excite his Admiration. Every where else Beauty pleases the Senses instead of surprising them, and creates sensual Desires, instead of commanding Respect. Thus the Face of *Fatima* attracted Admiration, while the rest of her Body gave Incitements only to Wantonness. The Union of her Neck and Shoulders was form'd by little and little, and as it were infensibly. Her alabaster Neck and her heaving Bosom seem'd to contain all the most precious Treasures of Youth. Her Hands and Arms were able to enchain the Universe. The Graces employ'd all their Skill in adorning every Part of this beautiful Body, and in giving Life and Motion to every Limb. If *Fatima* had wanted Wit, her superior Beauty was capable of hiding that Defect; but she had Wit in so high a Degree, that in hearing her speak one could hardly give any Attention to her Beauty. The Sweetness of her Humour, together with an agreeable and a winning Behaviour, gain'd her more Friends than her Beauty, and her Wit procur'd her more Admiration than Envy.

CHAP.

C H A P. III.

Of the Praise of BEAUTY.

THE First Physician grew so fond of the *Georgian* Lady, that whenever he left the Seraglio, he long'd to return back again to see her. He never was seized before with so violent a Passion. Such is the Effect of the Ambrosia drank in by the Eyes, that it inebriates the Mind, and lulls all the Senses. Whoever has a mind to be happy should never taste of this Liquor; or, if he does, he should always drink of it. The frequent Visits that *Abdeker* was obliged to make in the Seraglio gave him Opportunity of often seeing the lovely *Fatima*. One certain Evening it happen'd that the Doctor's Presence made such a deep Impression in the Mind of the charming Odalike, that she was surprized to find herself suddenly seized with an unusual Flame.

ABDEKER was young, and of a handsome and lovely Figure; his Mien was both engaging and commanded Respect; his Eyes were sparkling and full of Fire; he was of a tall and portly Stature; and his enchanting Voice procured him the Love and Confidence of all those that heard him speak. He was ardently officious in paying frequent Visits to *Fatima*; for Men are commonly forward in making their way to the Object they love. The great Inclination he had to please her added more Grace to his natural Beauty. At last he thus address'd her: Dear Madam, won't you pardon me for coming so

often

often to trouble you in your Solitude? I think of no other Happiness when I have the Pleasure of seeing you, and in your Absence I would give the World to enjoy your Company. You are, without doubt, one of those Flouries, whose Breath is sweeter than the refreshing Breezes of the Zephyrs, after gliding over spacious Plains adorned by *Phœbus* with aromatick Flowers, with fragrant Roses and sweet-smelling Thyme.

FATIMA blush'd. *Abdeker* remarking her Perplexity, after a Moment's Silence, spoke in these Terms: Madam, my Discourse ought not to alarm you; surely Heaven and Earth have concurr'd to make you the most lovely of all Mortals. Beauty is the most precious Gift that Nature can bestow on your Sex: It out-balances all the great Qualities that Men so vainly boast of. It mollifies the hardest Heart; it melts the Ice that chills the Fancy, and excites a gentle Heat. It raises a reasonable Passion, in a sober Man; it triumphs over the Strong, and animates the Weak; it humbles the Wise, and corrects the Senseless. It subdues the greatest Conquerors on Earth, who would perhaps think there could be no Limits put to their Power, if there were no female Conquerors to enchain them. It is by far more persuading than rhetorical Eloquence; it inspires honest Sentiments, the purest Morals, and brings along with it more convincing Proofs of the Existence of a God, than the most profound Philosopher can furnish. *Abdeker*, (replied *Fatima*) you sound the Praises of a very transitory Thing, that is subject to Changes, and may be easily lost. Beauty

is

is a Flower that buds out when *Aurora* unveils her
Eyes; it is caress'd by the Zephyrs; it attracts the
most charming Looks of shining *Phœbus*; it fades in
the Evening, and perishes under the silent Shades of
gloomy Night.   Madam, (replied the Doctor) your
Beauty is such that it will never fade: Besides, there
are Means to defend it against all Changes of Weather and Vicissitudes of Seasons; it may likewise be
protected against all the Insults and Threats of cruel
Distempers, that often disfigure the most lovely Face.
And creeping Old-Age, that ploughs the smoothest
Face, shall have no Power over yours.   A Physician
is as much obliged to give Precepts for the Preservation of Beauty, as he is for the preserving or recovering Health.   It is not sufficient that a Physician
should render himself useful only in preserving Life;
he is also obliged to endeavour to render that Life
agreeable, which he can can easily do, without acting inconsistently with the Gravity of his Profession.
What should we think of an Architect that should
employ all his Skill in raising us a lasting solid Building, without giving himself the least Trouble to
adorn it? He must have consider'd us as brutal Animals, that seek only to shelter themselves from the
Injuries of the Weather, and prefer Caves to the
most magnificent Palaces. Man, who is distinguish'd
from such Beings by a rational Soul, is of a more
delicate Taste; he knows how to embellish the most
necessary Things in Life, with some graceful Ornament.   He seasons his Provisions; he sleeps with
pleasure upon a Down Bed; he converts an uncul-
tivated Soil into pleasant Walks.   In a Word, he
                                             has

has the Art of turning every thing to his Pleasure and Advantage.

ABDEKER perceiving that the young Odalike listen'd to every thing he spoke with great Attention, continued in these Terms : There are (said he) two Kinds of Beauty, that of the Soul, and that of the Body. As it is the Philosopher's Business to preserve the first, so in like manner it is the Physician's Duty to use his utmost Endeavours to keep the second from any thing that may impair it. Both may be united together. The Beauty of the Body often discovers that of the Soul; but how often do we see Goodness and Greatness of Soul, with other noble Talents, lie hid under exterior Deformity ? When there is no Prejudice in the Case, the Beauty of the Body always prevails, and never misses to please. From hence may be understood the Advantage that a Physician has over a Moral Philosopher. I say, a Physician; for why should the Care of Beauty be separated from the Object of Physick ? For it always accompanies Health, and for many Reasons the one should concern us as much as the other. Therefore it is the Duty of all the Ministers of Health to know what may properly contribute to preserve Beauty, and to remove all those Defects that may render the Body deform'd; for the Remedies that are to be used in such Cases are so far from being hurtful to the Health, that on the contrary they are the surest and most impenetrable Shield we can oppose to the piercing Shafts of Pain and Distempers.

As you appear to me (replied *Fatima*) so positive about the Extent and Power of your Art, I desire
you

you to inftruct me in· fome of its Secrets. It is not
mere Curiofity that induces me to make fuch a De·
mand; it is rather the Defire that all living Beings
have of becoming happy.   Neither am I perfuaded
that Happinefs is founded upon a chimerical Princi·
ple, fince Health and Beauty are its only Bafis. Our
actual and interior Happinefs confifts in Health, and
our Self-Love makes us believe that Beauty is apt to
procure us the Efteem and Approbation of others.
It is upon thefe two Points that our relative Happinefs chiefly depends.   Therefore, learned *Abdeker*,
you will be pleafed to contribute to the Happinefs of
a Scholar that well knows the Value of your Art,
and that is refolved never to let flip an Opportunity
of giving you convincing Proofs of her fincere Acknowledgment.   I make you no Profeffions of my
Docility; for I prefume that a Woman will not be
difobedient, when the Point in queftion is to flatter
and fupport her Vanity, and procure her the Means
of pleafing, which is what the Sex chiefly aim at.
Farewel: Reflect upon the Object of my Demand,
and don't forget to come to fee me to-morrow Morn·
ing; for I expect to learn all thofe Myfteries in
Phyfick, that contribute to the Prefervation of
BEAUTY.

CHAP.

CHAP. IV.

Of the learned Dreams of ABDEKER.

*A*BDEKER never felt such violent Emotions as when he returned back to his Lodging. His doubting whether he had gained his Point or not, the Desire of pleasing, and the Hope of seeing very soon the Mistress of his Heart, tormented by turns his restless Mind. Besides, the Shame he felt for his Weakness, the Fear of displeasing *Mahomet*, the Certainty he had of being punished if the Sultan should know his Intrigues, and, in fine, the small Prospect of gaining *Fatima*, caused such Distraction and Trouble in his Mind, that he knew not what Measures to take. His Heart beat one while with Precipitation, another while stopp'd; yet soon after began to beat again with new Vigor, and then again suddenly ceased its Motion. Sleep was a Stranger to his Eyes, till the Stars had arrived at the midst of their Course: He then dreamt that several Phantoms suddenly rush'd into his Chamber; amongst whom he saw *Heraclides* of *Tarentum*, who after falling in Love with *Antiochis* dedicated a Treatise to her, for whom he had composed Cosmetics *. He saw also *Moschion* † and *Mercurialis* ‡, who both forged Arms

---

* See the History of Medicine by *Daniel le Clerc*, Part II. Book II. Chap. 7. and Part III. Book II. Chap. 2.

† *Le Clerc*, Part II. Book IV. Sect. i. Chap. 13.

‡ His Book is intituled, *De Decoratione, liber non solum medicis & philosophis, verùm etiam omnium disciplinarum studiosis*

in

in order to combat against the Defects that presumed
to attack the Graces. Among those Ghosts there
were some that kept in Chains the most hideous
Monsters. UGLINESS, with a squinting Eye, a
crooked Nose, a livid Complexion, ill-proportion'd
Members, and a large, ill-furnish'd, half-open'd
Mouth, was scorn'd by all, and trampled under their
Feet. *Abdeker*, unable any longer to endure the
Sight of so horrible a Spectre, roused himself up,
and endeavoured to calm the unruly Tempest of his
boisterous Imagination; and being more fatigued by
that Slumber than he would have been by the hardest Labour, he threw himself upon a Sopha, and
thought to repose for some Moments, but in a short
time Imagination began to plead for her former Pre-
rogatives. His Dreams, though more calm than
his former ones, kept nevertheless his Senses in such
a Degree of Tension, as was most proper to render
those Objects sensible to his Mind, whose Images he
had already form'd in his Brain. He fancied that
Circe appeared before him. *Circe* was the Daughter
of the *Sun:* She had so deep a Knowledge of the
Virtues of Plants, that she had experienced their
most wonderful Effects. *Medea*, her Niece, had the
Art to restore to Youth *Æson* her Stepfather. *Arte-
misia* * was Queen of *Caria:* Her Constancy and

apprimè utilis; *ex Hieron. Mercurialis, Medicinæ practicæ in
Gymnasio Patavino principem locum obtinentis, Explicationibus à
Julio Mancino excerptus.* Francofurti, 1587.

* Botanists pretend, that this Lady gave the Name of *Arte-
misia* to the Plant we call Mugwort. She lived 400 Years before *Cleopatra.*

Tenderness

Tenderneſs towards her Huſband *Mauſolus* will always remain a ſurpriſing Example to all Women of future Ages. *Cleopatra* *, that Queen of *Egypt* ſo remarkable for her Wit and Beauty, employ'd nevertheleſs all the Arts of Coquetry, in order to conquer *Cæſar* and enchain *Marc Antony. Aſpaſia* †, that handſome *Phocean* Lady, who inflamed the Hearts of two *Perſian* Kings, was ſo ſkill'd in the divine Art of Medicine, that ſhe has left to the Fair Sex a Collection of the choiceſt Precepts for the Preſervation both of Health and Beauty. He alſo believ'd that he ſaw *Olyroe, Epione, Egle* ‡, together with a great Train of Nymphs, who declared to him that they labour'd with the utmoſt Care to diſpatch whatever concerns the Embelliſhment of the Body; and that they invented a thouſand Schemes which took away or hide entirely the Imperfections and Deformities that happen either on accouut of Diſtempers, or by any other Cauſe whatſoever. He fancied that one of them whiſper'd to him, that *Fatima*'s Deſire to pleaſe proceeded from her wiſhing to conquer his Heàrt; and that, after their Example, ſhe ſhould make great Progreſs in an Art, the Principles of

---

* We have a Work that is intituled, *Cleopatræ Græcorum libri*, attributed to *Cleopatra*. Thoſe Books are very ancient; for *Galen* drew ſeveral Compoſitions from them, that belong to the Ornament of the Body, and he does not cite them as new. *Galen* lived 200 Years after *Cleopatra. Gal. de Comp. Medicam. local.* Lib. I. Cap. 1, 8. & Lib. IV. Cap. 7. *Paul Eginette, Ætius,* and ſeveral other Authors cite the ſame Books.

† In *Ætius* we find ſeveral Fragments of the Books of *Aſpaſia.*

‡ See the Hiſtory of Medicine, Part II. Book III. Ch. 13.

C which

which she defign'd to learn. We fhall admit her, faid fhe, into our Company, wherein fhe fhall be honour'd with the firft Dignity, and all the Prin-ceffes of the Earth fhall look upon her Counfels as fo many Oracles.

ABDEKER, at this Conjuncture, thought he faw his charming Odalike. I know no greater Hap-pinefs, faid he, my lovely *Fatima*, than to have it in my Power to fatisfy your Requeft: I will ufe my utmoft Endeavour to anfwer the Confidence thou haft placed in me. Scarce had he utter'd thefe Words, when he rofe up, that he might proftrate himfelf at the Feet of his adorable *Fatima*; but he found nothing to grafp but a Shadow. At his Emo-tion Sleep fled from him, together with the Fantoms that feemed to flutter around him.

At this Time the Sun afcended above the Hori-zon, and the Hour was at hand when he was to enter the Seraglio, and to pay his Refpects to the Darling of his Heart. He called his Slaves, and order'd them to bring him every thing that might render his Garments magnificent. He took the Suit of Cloaths that became him beft; he chofe the Tur-ban that gave him the moft fweet and noble Air. He never in his Life took fo much Pains to drefs himfelf. Every thing belonging to his Attire was as much ftudied, as that of a Bridegroom when con-ducted to the Temple of *Hymen*.

CHAP.

CHAP. V.

Of the Invention of the TOILET.

*F*ATIMA pafs'd the Night as uneafily as her
Lover. The Picture of *Abdeker* was fo deeply
engraved in her Imagination, that it prefented itfelf
to her Mind more than a hundred times a Day.
Her Soul, that till then had only felt fweet and
pleafing Paffions, began to be hurried on by the
moft violent Agitations. As fhe was going to Bed
fhe thought of her Doctor, and when fhe awoke he
was the Object of her firft Ideas. Her Sleep was
fhorter than ufual. This Morning fhe faw *Aurora*
opening the Gates of the Eaft, and heard her pro-
claiming the Approach of the brilliant Star of Day.

SURPRISED by the panting Motions of her Heart,
and hurried on by a fond Paffion of which fhe was
no way Miftrefs, fhe cried out, *Fatima* is conquer'd!
She loves, and it is an Effect of Sympathy. Yes,
I know thee, thou unexpected Impulfe of Nature,
by thy Livelinefs and thy invincible Force. O lovely
Cupid, I fhall not fight againft thee! Strike *Abdeker*
with the fame Arrow with which thou haft wounded
me; and after fo doing I will erect to Thee, to thy
Mother, and to BEAUTY, an Altar *, upon which
I will burn the fweeteft Perfumes. My Intention in
erecting this Altar is to make all Men fenfible, not
only of thy Value, O BEAUTY! but alfo of the Honour and Worfhip that are due to thee. Thou fhalt

* The TOILET.

fee

fee that I will not fail to render thee my Homage
every Morning, and that I fhall be careful in remo-
ving all the Defects that may attack a Face upon
which thou haft difplay'd fome of thy Charms:
That every fair Lady through all Parts of the World
may erect thee an Altar after my Example; and
that, during the Solemnization of thy Myfteries,
may be excluded as profane Wretches, the Indifcreet,
the Jealous, the Impertinent, and the Senfelefs:
That Lovers alone may be admitted to fing their
Amours, and to vent before thy Shrine a thoufand
Sighs, and fteal a thoufand Favours: That every
Part of this Altar may manifeft the Power of *Cupid,
Venus,* and BEAUTY.

THEN immediately approaching a Table of Cedar, that ftood in her Chamber, fhe cover'd it with
a Cloth of *Tyrian* Purple, upon which fhe fpread
the Veil that cover'd her Head.   Afterwards fhe
placed in the Middle a portable Looking-glafs,
which a *Venetian* Ambaffador gave as a Prefent to
Mahomet.   She placed on each Side of this Glafs
two round Boxes, which contained the moft excellent Powder that could be found in the Ifland of *Cyprus.*   The Front was garnifh'd with China Veffels,
that contained the moft fragrant Pomatum that *Italy*
could afford.   In the fame Rank were placed feveral Flaggons of the fweeteft and moft exquifite
Quinteffence, together with the moft precious Perfumes of all the Eaft.   In fine, behind the Glafs
fhe placed two fmall Boxes, that were found in the
'Temple of *Paphos;* one of which contain'd the
Combs ufed by *Venus,* and the other was fill'd with
                                                    fome

some Leaves of Romances with which the Lovers of former Times were wont to curl the Locks of their Mistresses Hair, whenever they sought to mitigate their Cruelty, or render their Hearts more sensible: And all these Ornaments were slightly cover'd over with a thin Veil of Crimson Silk.

FATIMA applauded herself for her Invention, and resolved to be the first Priestess of her Altar. She immediately made choice of the Ornaments that were to be worn by every Lady that was willing to offer Vows and Incense to BEAUTY. She put on over her Robe a white Cimarre, that was very short and had large Sleeves. She took off the Fillet that tied her Hair. and let her Locks wave carelesly in Ringlets over her Breast and Shoulders. She might then have been taken for one of those Virgins who are appointed to guard the eternal Fire consecrated to the Goddess *Vesta.* She sat opposite her Work, that she might the better observe it. She ranged some Locks of Hair that covered too much of her Forehead, and joined them with the Rose and the Jessamine. *Abdeker* in the mean time enter'd her Apartment, and, notwithstanding the studied Compliment he thought to make her, found himself unable to testify his Love and Respect otherwise than by prostrating himself at her Feet; for Love struck him dumb. *Fatima*, in order to cover her Confusion, smiled at the Doctor, who, in approaching her, put on as assured a Countenance as he was able, and at last addressed her in these Terms, and thus revealed the whole Cause of the Trouble of his Mind.

LOVELY

LOVELY *Fatima*, you defire, after the Example of *Cleopatra* and *Afpafia*, to dive into the inner Secrets of Medicine. Thofe illuftrious Women were taught by the Phyficians every thing that concern'd Beauty. They fpent all their leifure Hours at this ufeful Study: But as you are handfomer, and have much more Wit than they, you will undoubtedly make a greater Progrefs. Their Phyfician never acted his Part with fo much Pleafure and Candour as I will. The Sentiments you infpire are —— He fuddenly ftopp'd: He perceived that he was going to make a Declaration of Love, in a Place wherein it was Death for any one except the Emperor to make any fuch Declaration.

FATIMA feemed to take no Notice of what he faid, for fear of being obliged to complain of a Difcourfe that gave her fo much Satisfaction. She immediately refumed the Difcourfe, as if fhe heard nothing of what was fpoke. Well, *Abdeker*, faid fhe, am I not this Day to learn the firft Leffons of your Art? Perform your Promife, I will liften to you very attentively.

C H A P. VI.

The FIRST LESSON.

ALTHOUGH I don't doubt of your Penetration and Capacity, replied *Abdeker*, yet I fhall endeavour to render my Inftructions fo plain and methodical,

methodical, that there shall be no Room for Objections. Besides, I will avoid all tedious Repetitions, that can inform you of nothing that is new.

BEAUTY is that Form of an entire Body, which pleases every one of our Senses. This entire Body pleases our Eyes by the Extent, Colour, Number, Disposition, and Proportion of its Parts: It pleases our Sense of Feeling by its Texture, our Nose by its Smell, and our Hearing by its Sound. May I presume to say, that you are the Model of what I have defin'd?

To return to each of these Parts. 1. I say that the Form of an entire Body, that can be consider'd as beautiful, ought to please our Eyes by its Extent. If a Person be too big or too little, too fat or too lean, we cannot like him, because there is not a certain Resemblance or Proportion between him and us, or between the Generality of Mankind. For this Reason we charge Nature with Extravagance, when we consider the Size of a Giant; and when we see a Dwarf, we blame her for being too sparing, or too forgetful. A beautiful Body is conformable to the general Rule, that Nature alone has prescribed.

2. THE Colour of the Parts is one of the Articles that Nature should observe in the Composition of a handsome Body; and if a fair Skin is a Perfection, one that is brown, yellowish, and cover'd with Freckles, is to be accounted ugly.

3. THE Number of Parts that compose an entire Body is so determined, that it neither can increase nor diminish without a remarkable Deformity. Imagine

gine a Man with two Nofes and one Eye, would not fuch a Face appear very ftrange? For we fee that the Want of the Eyebrows, a Wen on the Forehead, a Wart, a Pimple, or any fuch Excrefcence, makes a very difagreeable Impreffion.

4. BEAUTY confifts in the Difpofition of the Parts. Ill-ranged Teeth, or Locks of Hair flovenly placed upon the Forehead, render the whole Countenance fo odd that it cannot pleafe, let the other Parts be ever fo handfome.

5. THERE ought to be an exact Proportion between all the Parts; for what feems more ridiculous than a great Head upon a fmall Body, and a fmall Nofe upon a great Face?

I SAY, in the fecond Place, that the perfe t Texture of the Parts is abfolutely neceffary towards the Formation of Beauty. A rough Skin, cover'd over with Hair and Pimples, and deeply mark'd with the Small Pox, is equally difpleafing to the Touch and to the Eye.

THIRDLY, Our Senfe of Smelling ought to be fatisfied in the Enjoyment of thofe Things we account to be beautiful: For a Perfon that has a ftrong Breath, or that emits bad Smells from the other Parts of his Body, difgufts all that approach him.

IN fhort, a pleafing harmonious Voice is a neceffary Accomplifhment in a beautiful Woman, fince it is the beft Means fhe can make ufe of, in difpofing of the Hearts that are captivated by the lovely Features of her Body. I knew a beautiful Lady, who fcarcely had one Admirer, becaufe fhe had a rude

and

and uncouth Voice. Every one drew near to see her, but retired after he had heard her speak.

I THINK the Idea you give me of Beauty, replied the young Odalike, is very exact, and your Definition is so general, that it is applicable to all Beauties of any Kind whatsoever: And indeed I expected nothing less from the Brightness of your Wit, and the Clearness of your Ideas. But perhaps I did ill to interrupt you: Be pleased to go on; for I believe what you have advanced requires a further Explanation, and that it is but a Plan of the Method you design to follow.

YOUR Approbation, replied the Doctor, is the most prevailing Motive to induce me to do well. Besides, while I am inspired with the Desire of pleasing you, can I fail of Success? As to what concerns my present Undertaking, you ought rather to praise me for this sincere Desire, than for my Performance. To be brief, I shall make no other Apology than to assure you that I will obey your Orders.

C H A P. VII.

Of EXTENSION, *consider'd as it regards* BEAUTY.

MAGNITUDE in general has three Dimensions, to wit, Length, Breadth, and Depth; and each of these may be defective.

ACCORDING

ACCORDING to our Forefathers, the moſt beautiful Height of a Man conſiſted in four Cubits *; ſo that one was accounted too tall or too low, in proportion as he was higher or lower than this Meaſure.

AN exceſſive Height depends for the moſt part on the Parents, on the Climate, on the Education, on the Food a Child takes in his Infancy, and on certain Exerciſes. All theſe Cauſes may concur together to produce the aforeſaid Effect. It is probable that it might be prevented; but, when it is once produced, all the Power of Medicine cannot in the leaſt deſtroy it.

A LOW Stature depends not only on the aforeſaid Cauſes, but alſo on a vicious Conformation of the inferior Parts, and on certain Diſorders. What I have ſaid about Length may be alſo underſtood of Depth. When the Eyes are too much ſunk into the Head, I believe there is no Remedy in Art capable of rendering them more prominent. Nevertheleſs you ſhall find, in the Principles which I intend to eſtabliſh, a certain Connection between Cauſes and Effects; ſo that it will happen ſometimes, that in deſtroying a general Ailment, we alſo deſtroy a particular Defect. Thus, after curing a general Leanneſs, the Cavities that were about the *Claviculæ* diſappear; and the empty Spaces, which occaſioned the Collar-Bones to appear too far advanced, are fill'd up with Fleſh. You will not ſuſpect me of preſuming to talk to you of the Breadth of certain Parts,

* This Meaſure may be reduced to about five Foot and a half.

which

which a Naturalist might name without a Blush. Such a Relation would alarm your Modesty; and I ought to respect the Veil with which Decency has cover'd that sacred Place *. At present I am to speak to you only of the Breadth of an entire Body, with its Relation to the other Parts of the Whole. If the Body be too plump and full, it is reckon'd to be too fat; on the contrary we reckon it to be lean, when it is not in that Degree of Fatness that the Ornament of the whole Body requires. I shall proceed to examine each of these Particulars.

C H A P. VIII.

Of excessive FATNESS.

THE Skin is not the only Covering of the Body; it is likewise wrapp'd up with the Membrane of the Fat. This Membrane is composed of an infinite Number of Cells, that communicate with each other. It adheres very close to the Skin it accompanies throughout all Parts of the Body, fills up all the intermediate Spaces of the Muscles, and passes through all the Circumvolutions of the Viscera. These Cells are fill'd up with an oily Matter, which can enter into the Blood, and repair its Loss in the Time of long Abstinence. It keeps the Muscles constantly supple, and of consequence fit for the Action for which Nature has de-

* See OBSERVATION the First.

sign'd

fign'd them. It defends the Body from the too great
Impreffion it would otherwife receive from the Cold,
which is always more felt by lean People than by
fat. Its principal Ufe, in regard of the Subject I
treat of, is to plump the Skin, and fill the intermediate Spaces of the Mufcles; for by that means its
Surface becomes fmooth and agreeable to the Eye.
The beft-limb'd and beft-featur'd Body becomes deform'd, without an exact and neceffary Proportion
of Fat. Fatnefs may be in too great a Quantity,
and that Kind of Fatnefs may be general or particular. It may be alfo in too fmall a Quantity,
which I fhall defcribe in fpeaking of Leannefs.

C H A P. IX.

Of too much FATNESS in general.

IN general too much Fatnefs fpoils Beauty; for
it effaces all thofe fine Features, which Nature
draws with fuch Art and Delicacy. It thickens the
Neck, which under its natural Form excites both
Love and Affection; but by the huge Bulk it acquires by Fatnefs, it caufes Difguft. It deftroys that
graceful Stature, which promifes the moft fweet and
the moft delicate Pleafures. It deprives the Members of that Activity and Nimblenefs, which feduces
the Senfes by their lively and agreeable Motions.
The great Sloth and Careleffnefs, which appear in
all the Actions of thofe that are exceffively fat, either tire or lull afleep the Spectator. What a furprifing

prifing Bulk was that Woman, whom Hiftory has
inform'd us was fix hundred Pound Weight! What
Comparifon can be made between her and that
light-footed Nymph, who hardly leaves the Print of
her Feet in the Sand as fhe runs along?

ONE is apt to believe that Perfons in this Cafe are
robuft, and in perfect Health. On the contrary,
they are ftupid; their Apprehenfion is not fo lively
as it naturally ought to be; they breathe with Difficulty, and are fubject to frequent Diftempers. They
have alfo a certain Incapacity of Breeding, fo that
Women of that Complexion are commonly barren.
The Soul is overwhelm'd with the Weight of a huge
Lump of Matter, and all the Functions of the Un-
derftanding are in fuch a languifhing Condition, that
it can fhew no Marks of its former Brightnefs. If
all thefe Motives were not fufficient to engage Men
to make a ftrict Enquiry into the Caufes and Remedies of fuch an Inconvenience, I think this one only
Motive founded upon Experience fhould neceffarily
determine them, namely, that thofe who are too fat
do not live fo long as others.

THE firft Caufe of Fatnefs proceeds from the too
great Quantity of nourifhing Particles with which the
Blood abounds.

THE fecond Caufe is the too great Force of the
Stomach, and all the other Organs that help Digeftion. It is wrong to attribute all to the Quality
of the Food; for we fee that fome People become
very fat by living upon Food that contains but very
little Nourifhment.

D   THE

THE remote Caufes are every thing that contributes to preferve Life, and which, by ufing it after a certain Manner, may difpofe for a general Fatnefs. Such as, for Example, is the Air when too cold and too moiſt; the Food that contains too much Juice; Drink that furniſhes too much Nouriſhment; Want of Exercife; too much Sleep; the Suppreſſion of fome Excretion, and a perfeƈt Calm of all the Paſſions.

I REMEMBER, replied *Fatima*, that I have read in the Memoirs of fome Travellers, that the Northern People are commonly too fat and too big, whereas thofe that live nearer the Sun are commonly too lean and wither'd. This Difference depends upon Perfpiration, which is always greater in a hot and dry Climate, than in a cold and moiſt Country. I believe the Relation of thofe Travellers the more readily, becaufe I have conſtantly obferved that Cattle are fatter in Winter than in Summer.

I REMEMBER alfo to have read in the Memoirs of the fame Travellers, that in fome Provinces of *Europe*, where the Inhabitants make immoderate Ufe of Beer, thick Wine, and Liquors that contain much Nouriſhment, fuch People are generally very fat. You fee, dear *Abdeker*, that I know how to turn every thing to the Advantage of your Syſtem, and that all my Ideas tend to authorife what you advance. But I can give you a more convincing Proof upon this Subjeƈt.

You know *Zaira* the Wife of *Calil* Pacha; ſhe had one of thofe handfome little Faces which feduce, though they contain nothing that can be call'd regu-

lar

lar Beauty. These two Years paſt ſhe has led the
moſt idle, the moſt luxurious, and the moſt eaſy Life
of any Woman in her Station. She paſſes two
Thirds of her Life in her Bed, and the other Third
on the Sopha. She feeds upon the moſt nouriſhing
Food that can be found; but this good while paſt
ſhe has taken a Frolick to live upon Milk, Eggs,
Broths and Jellies made of the moſt tender Animals.
She equally abhors Work and every Kind of Food
that would load her Stomach, and chuſes what ſhe
can eaſily digeſt. Now *Zaira* is become ſo fat, that
one cannot diſcover the leaſt Feature of thoſe that
Nature drew upon her Face; ſhe perfectly repreſents
the rough Draught of a Statue.

O HAPPY would Maſters be, anſwer'd *Abdeker,*
if all their Diſciples were as tractable as you! Permit me to tell you, that you have forgot, in the De-
ſcription you have given, one of the principal Cauſes
of which I made mention. As you have always
been brought up in Innocence, you could not as yet
reflect upon certain Circumſtances of Life, which
contribute to promote Fatneſs. There is a Kind of
Liquor filter'd in our interior Parts, which is the Ba-
ſis of all our Vigour; it is the Source of that Pleaſure and of that Bliſs we perceive when we pay our
Reſpects to a lovely Object. This Liquor conſumes
us like Fire if it be too active, or if it abounds in
too great a Quantity: But if the Heat it cauſes be
moderate, and if we uſe it ſparingly, the Body becomes fat inſenſibly, and the Mind is ſecured againſt
ſuch violent Paſſions as might deſtroy Fatneſs. The
ſame Thing happens, when the Principle of that in-

born

born Fire is quite extinguifh'd. The Soul and Body lofe that Vigour which characterifes the Beings who fully enjoy all the Perfections of their Exiftence. It is by deftroying the Principle of this Fire, that we render more fat and tender the Animals we defign for the Table. It is the Want of that vital Fire which caufes fuch Sloth and Fatnefs in thofe Monfters that the Emperor has intrufted to guard you.

I own, replied *Fatima*, that I have not given an exact Account of all the Caufes that produce immoderate Fatnefs: But now an Object of greater Confequence excites my Curiofity. I would fain know the Method you would take to prevent the like Caufes, and the Remedies you would employ to deftroy the Effects they have produced. Let us fuppofe, for an Inftant, that *Zaira* came to afk your Advice, what would you prefcribe for her?

In order to *Zaira's* being perfectly cured, anfwer'd the Doctor, there are two principal Things to be done: The firft is obtain'd by a Food that contains a fmall Quantity of Nourifhment; the fecond confifts in diminifhing the immoderate Quantity of nourifhing Particles that are already mix'd with her Blood.

To remove the firft Caufe, I would confine *Zaira* to a very ftrict Diet; that is, I would diminifh by degrees the Quantity of Food fhe is accuftom'd to take every Day; for all fudden Changes are dangerous. Befides, I would carefully examine the Quality of her Food, and make her frequently eat falt Meat and Spices; and order her alfo to make ufe of fuch Pulfe as contains little Nourifhment, and con-

tributes

tributes to keep the Body open. I would perhaps engage her to eat more Meat than Bread. Pacha *Mazoul*'s Wife ufed this Means with Succefs. Naturalifts have always obferved, that fuch Fowls as live upon Prey, and continually eat Flefh, are always leaner than thofe that feed upon Vegetables. Befides, I would order her to take nothing for her Supper, but a fmall Collation of dry or preferv'd Fruit. Hitherto I have impofed no fevere Penance upon *Zaira:* But perhaps fhe would think me too fevere, if I order'd her to fleep little, and to quit that foft Bed on which fhe with fo much Pleafure repofes her Limbs, that are fatigued only with refting too long; if I order'd her to walk often, and in the warmeft Hour of the Day, and to accuftom herfelf to certain Exercifes which fhe imagines are fit only for her Slaves, though they are very neceffary for reftoring her Beauty; if I order'd her from time to time to give full Reins to her Reflections, that fhe might in fo doing know herfelf and alfo them that are about her. Such Orders would certainly make *Zaira* fall into a Paffion.

I do not know, replied the lovely *Fatima*, whether fhe would be at the Expence of fuch Remedies as you prefcribe for her. I think I heard that fhe avoided even the Shadow of Fatigue. So much the worfe for herfelf, anfwer'd *Abdeker* fmiling; for I thought fhe would make ufe of the Means I prefcribed for curing her. Phyficians do not always cure by Words. But *Zaira* may do what fhe thinks proper; at leaft if fhe does not obferve the Diet I order for her, fhe muft have Recourfe to the Reme-

dies that anſwer the ſecond Intention. I give you
my Word, ſhe will ſoon grow lean, if ſhe ſubmits
to the Power of Medicine. You laugh in your Turn.
Yes, replied *Fatima*; I think I ſee a Phyſician walk
in the middle of a Croud of conſumptive and hectic
People, whoſe Meals conſiſt of nothing but ſome
Apozems and a ſmall Quantity of Chicken-Broth.
I'll warrant you the Doctor won't fatten them.

I LIKE, ſays *Abdeker*, to ſee you diverted by ſo
ſerious a Subject: I am perſuaded you will not be
much amuſed by the Remainder of what I have to
tell you. You will perhaps reproach me for a Jar-
gon that is peculiar to Phyſicians alone, and that has
been oftentimes reckon'd obſcure and barbarous:
Nevertheleſs they muſt need have Terms to expreſs
whatever belongs to their Art. Are not you permitted to give different Names to your Gowns and
Head-dreſſes, according as they have more or leſs
Folds?

I SAY that, in order to free the Blood from too
great a Quantity of nouriſhing Juices, all the Excretions muſt be increaſed; which will be effected
by Purges, Diuretics, and Diaphoretics.

PURGES carry off not only the thick Humours
that clog the Stomach and the Lower Belly, but alſo a great Quantity of the Humours that are proper
for the Increaſe and Nouriſhment of the human Body. By their Acrimony and ſtimulating Faculty
they irritate the Glands of the Inteſtines, and force
them as it were to filtre a new Quantity of Lymph
and Mucus, that may ſupply the Defect of what
they loſt.

ONE may procure a great Excretion of Urine by giving the light Aperitives, such as Maidenhair; and by using the Acids of Vegetables, such as Limonade, Verjuice, Gooseberries, the Juice of Oranges and Lemons, Pomegranates, and the Fruit of the Barberry Tree. We reckon Vinegar as a great Specifick for causing Leanness; and Experience demonstrates evidently that it never fails to produce that Effect, let it be used in what Manner soever.

I KNEW a Quack in *Arabia* that made *Zaira* a Present of a Box full of candied Kernels of Cherry-stones. Such a Gift should not be despised, nor consider'd as one of those elegant Trifles that are usually presented to Children; for long Experience proves that the Kernels of Cherry-stones are very diuretic. Some People pretend that they expel the Gravel, and break the Stones that are form'd in the Reins.

I PROPOSE, in the third Place, to increase Perspiration, and even to make her sweat; for Experience shews, that those who use much Exercise, and who of consequence perspire in Proportion, never become too fat. Besides, we see that fat People, who lead a sedentary Life, soon become lean when they embrace a Way of living that requires Exercise and Labour. This is what happen'd to *Zaira:* As long as she lived in the midst of Plenty, she was so delicate that she could hardly walk. She order'd herself to be carried in a Litter, that People might know that her Fatness was proportional to her Riches, and to the Number of her Slaves. Her Husband died six Months ago; he was over Head

and

and Ears in Debt, and was out of favour with the
Grand Signior. She was obliged to deliver all her
Goods to the Creditors ; and being forced to get her
Livelihood by the Sweat of her Brow, she loft all
her Fat, and recover'd her Health.

WELL, *Zaira* is cured, as you pretend, replied
the young Odalike. There is one Thing furprizes
me in that Cure; I cannot conceive how you could
perform it without Bleeding. Is not fuch a Method
contrary to the Practice of *Æfculapius?* Can a Perfon believe that he is thoroughly cured without ufing
that Remedy? Your ironical Speech, anfwer'd the
Doctor, againft a Remedy fo univerfally employ'd,
will not hinder me from anfwering your Objection.
I knew that fome Practitioners order frequent Bleeding in the prefent Cafe; becaufe in taking a certain
Quantity of Blood, they take away the Overplus of
Nourifhment that overcharges the Body. I admit
Bleeding is proper according to their Syftem; but
the Effect that refults from it is quite different from
their Intention : For Bleeding, by retarding the Motion of the Fluids, and diminifhing the Force of the
Solids, occafions the nourifhing Part of the Lymph
to ftay longer than ordinary in the Veffels. It is
for this Reafon that the Country Farmers (who are
always very induftrious in every thing that tends to
their Profit) commonly bleed their Swine, when they
have a mind to fatten them with more Speed and
with more Succefs. The *Arabians,* before they turn
out their Horfes to Grafs, bleed them about the
Month of *May,* that they may fatten the fooner.
For my part, I like much better the Opinion of thofe
who

who in the like Cafes excite an artificial Fever, which, by accelerating the Circulation of the Blood, and by ſtimulating all the Fibres, expels the ſuperfluous Humours, and frees the Body from that uſeleſs Load, which was the Product of ſeveral Years.

I am ſo pleaſed with your Way of Reaſoning, replied *Fatima* to the Doctor, that I am tempted to propoſe you new Objections: But I chuſe in the mean time to pray you to keep your Word, and tell me the Reaſon why ſome Parts of the Body become fat more than the reſt. Fulfil your Promiſe, whilſt the Principles you have laid down are freſh in my Memory.

CHAP. X.

Of exceſſive FATNESS in particular.

IT often happens in Men as well as Women, continued *Abdeker*, that one Part of the Body fattens more than any of the reſt. The Breaſts and Belly are generally ſubject to become very bulky. It is the general Cauſes, of which I have ſpoken to you, that produce this Effect: But in Women ſeveral accidental Cauſes contribute to raiſe a Swelling in thoſe Parts. A Woman is big-bellied when ſhe is with Child, and ſometimes by the Accidents that happen after her Delivery: Her Breaſts at the ſame time ſwell with Milk. But as theſe particular Caſes require much Explanation, and oblige the Phyſician

to

to a great deal of Precaution, you will permit me to pafs over their Theory in Silence, and only to make mention of the Effects that refult from the general Caufes which produce exceffive Fatnefs.

I once faw a Woman whofe Belly was two Ells in Circumference: She could fcarce walk, and drag along the enormous Weight of her Body. Some Friends advifed her to carry about her Middle a Girdle of Salt, that is, a Girdle fo contrived as to contain Salt. As this Advice feem'd very eafy to be put in Execution, fhe follow'd it exactly, and grew fo lean in a fhort Time, that fhe could hardly be known. Her Belly was two Thirds lefs than before, and her Body recover'd that Agility which is requifite for the Prefervation of Health and Beauty. This Succefs furprifed all thofe who were Witneffes thereof; though there is nothing in it fo miraculous, but it may be accounted for. The fimple Application of common Salt is very efficacious for diffolving the Humours that are 'condenfed by remaining too long in the Glands. It is by its Ufe that Phyficians often liquefy the prodigious Tumors that feem to join the Chin to the Breaft.

The *European* Women feem to have more Means at hand to hinder their Bellies from growing big, than thofe of *Afia* or other Eaftern Countries. The Eaftern Women do not endeavour to mend their Shapes by ufing Garments that are too ftrait; whereas the *European* Women make ufe of Stays and Bodice that are ftiffen'd with Whalebone. This Kind of Drefs diminifhes the Capacity of the Lower Belly, obliges a Woman to ftand upright, to keep out

her

her Breaft and draw in her Shoulders, and gives her Stature and her Shape a particular Grace.

Women that are too fat have their Breafts too foft and bulky, hanging down like Bags. For your part, lovely *Fatima*, you were born in a Country where the Ladies do not fear this Inconveniency. The Women of *Georgia*, *Mingrelia*, and *Circaffia*, have their Breafts even in their Old Age as firm as the *European* Women have them in the Bloom of Youth. I have read in fome Author of Women whofe Breafts grew to fuch a Size, that they were obliged to make ufe of Strings. to keep them up, and Bandages to contract their Bulk.

It is thus that the Foot, bound up in a narrow Babouche * from Infancy, becomes fo pretty that it excites Defires in a Man, though he be not in the leaft amorous. Some Phyficians pretend that Balm pounded and applied to the Breafts hinders them from growing big; and *Pliny* afferts what Experience confirms, that the Fifh *Efquadre* applied to the Bouzolas † leffens them fo much by its aftringent Quality, that they become like the Breafts of a young Virgin. There are feveral other Remedies that are fpecific in this Cafe; but they are all Aftringents, and only differ as their aftringent Quality is greater or fmaller.

I told you that the Breafts may be kept within due Bounds by the fame Method that the Foot is prevented from growing. It is a Fact that is confirm'd by Experience. During Youth we may give

---

* A Kind of Slipper.   † Large hanging Breafts.

the

the Foot any determin'd Size we pleafe. I believe the natural Love that moft Men have for fmall Feet is founded upon a certain Principle of Delicacy. A long Foot moft commonly denotes a Perfon of mean Extraction, and that fhe was accuftom'd to hard Labour, and was quite carelefs of all that contributes to compleat Beauty. On the contrary, there is nothing fo enticing as fmall Feet, with a neat Pair of Shoes and Stockings.

You will permit me to tell you upon this Subject the Hiftory of *Rhodope*. This famous Courtefan built one of the Pyramids of *Egypt*, and left it as a ftately Monument of the great Number of her Lovers, and of the Excefs of their Liberality. It is faid that as fhe was one Day bathing herfelf in the *Nile*, (for fhe was of *Naucratis*, a City of *Egypt*) an Eagle carried off one of her Shoes to *Memphis*, and let it fall upon the Knees of the King, who, according to the Cuftom of the Country, was then adminiftring Juftice in the publick Square. The King, furprifed at fuch a Prodigy, and admiring the Beauty of the Foot by the Shape of the Shoe, fent Meffengers to make Enquiry after the Owner of it throughout his Dominions, with ftrict Orders to bring the Woman who had the Fellow of it. *Rhodope* was found to be the Perfon. As foon as fhe was brought before the King, he offer'd her his Hand and his Crown.

I THINK that fmall Foot, replied *Fatima*, walk'd very faft to great Fortune. Your Foot alfo, continued the Doctor, is one of thofe that are to tread upon the Throne. Flowers and Pleafures are to fpring where you ftand, and the Gods themfelves

perhaps

perhaps would be glad to have the Liberty of be-coming your Slaves.

You do not speak the Language of *Bubikir* *, re-plied *Fatima* smiling. Your Wit is not yet rusty by the Study of your Art; you have preserved the gen-teel Carriage of an amiable Man. But it is time for you to take your Rest. I expect you will come to-morrow to explain all the Principles of Lean-ness. The Doctor, after thanking the beautiful Odalike for the good Opinion she had of him, took leave of her and retired. After parting he found himself more inflamed by her Charms than ever he was before.

CHAP. XI.

A Description of LEANNESS.

*A*BDEKER did not fail coming again at the appointed Hour; for the Time seem'd very long whilst he was out of the Sight of *Fatima*. Par-don me, beautiful Odalique, says he, if the Subject I am going to treat of will furnish your Imagination with no chearful Ideas. It is yourself that obliges me to speak. I had hardly turn'd my Eyes towards LEANNESS, when I beheld a Representation of *Fa-*

---

* *Bubikir Zachary Errasa*, an *Arabian*, the Father of *Rha-sis*, a famous Physician, who wrote many Things relating to Medicine. He had great Reputation in *Turky* in the Time of *Mahomet*.

E   *mine,*

mine, *Envy*, and *Jealousy*. I saw the Hag lock'd up
in a dark Cavern, breathing a most infectious Àir,
having nothing else for Food and Nourishment.
When the Body is lean, the Face grows long, the
Eyes are sunk into the Head, the Mouth enlarges,
the Cheeks are hollow, the Face is pale, often yellow, and sometimes of the Colour of Lead; the
Bones are prominent, and seem to be almost out of
Joint; the Breast exhibits a dismal Representation of
a Vault, wherein one may count all the Arches; and
the spindle Shanks seem hardly able to sustain the
Bones of this walking Skeleton. It is a Spectre
which strikes all that look on it with Horror. If
the Person was fat before he grew lean, the Skin
grows wrinkled, the Fibres become soft and lax, and
the Parts which we desire should appear plump and
firm present nothing to the Eye but a displeasing ill-
shaped Figure, whose Surface is cover'd over with a
thousand Folds and Wrinkles, such as usually attend
on decrepit Old Age.

STOP, *Abdeker*, says *Fatima* interrupting him; this
Picture is too hideous, examine it no longer. Let
us rather see whether there be any Remedies for so
miserable a State; for I much pity Women of Sense
whose Features are in such a deplorable Condition.

THEY are commonly Women of the greatest Sense,
replied the Doctor, that are most subject to this Diforder. This you will easily conclude from the Se-
quel of our Discourse. Let us not confound our
Ideas, but let us dive into the Source of so many
Evils.

C H A P.

CHAP. XII.

Of a general LEANNESS.

GEneral Leanness is that State of the Body wherein the Fat is quite vanished, not only from under the Skin, but also from all the intermediate Spaces of the Muscles. This happens whenever the Cells of the Fatty Membrane are deprived of the Oil that should fill them. In this Case they sink and fall one upon another, and hardly leave any Signs of their Existence. The Causes that produce this Disorder are quite opposite to those that produce Fatness.

THE first Cause is the Want of a sufficient Quantity of nourishing Particles in the Blood ; the second is a particular Weakness in the Organs of Digestion. The remote Causes are the Non-Naturals, which either fail to furnish a sufficient Quantity of Nourishment, or contribute to the wasting of what is already acquired.

AS for those Disorders that produce a general Leanness, such as Ulcers of the Lungs, Obstructions of the Viscera in the Dropsy, an Abscess of the Liver in Hectics, we should be speedy in the Application of the most efficacious Remedies ; for in such Circumstances it is Health and Life, not Beauty, that call for our Assistance.

BUT the frightful State that I have described may exist, though there be no sensible Alteration in the Health. The *Ethiopians*, who live in a hot and dry

E 2   Climate,

Climate, are commonly very lean. Labourers also, who work hard during the Heat of the Day, and live upon coarse Diet, are very seldom fat. Likewise young Men, that are too much given to Women, have always a pale and disfigured Countenance. Add to these such as are too passionate, or who have too lively an Imagination; for they are commonly very lean.

I WAS acquainted in *Arabia* with the Daughter of a rich Sangiac *, whose Name was *Zelide*. The Tranquillity of her Heart and Mind was painted upon her Face, together with the Colours of Roses and Lilies. Her fat and fresh-colour'd Complexion attracted the Eyes of the whole City. She only perceived the Love she had for a certain young Man, by the Uneasiness she felt whenever she parted from him. This young Man's Name was *Hali*; she saw him every Day; he gain'd her Heart by a sweet and courteous Behaviour, and by the Sharpness of his Wit. *Hali* was employ'd in the Army, wherein he had already gone through the most confiderable Posts. A War declared against the King of *Persia* obliged him to be ready to take the Field upon the first Orders he should receive from the *Ottoman* Porte. He had enjoy'd so much Happiness in living along with *Zelide*, that he dreaded nothing so much as the Approach of the Spring, which was the Time he was to begin his Campaign. His Courage naturally led him to great Actions; but he could not without Regret lose Sight of *Zelide*, whom he loved so tenderly, and from whom he daily received innumerable

* A Governor of a Province.

Proofs

Proofs of sincere Friendship. He was so much pleased
in the Enjoyment of such a lovely Creature, that he
could by no means resolve to abandon her to any
Rival whatsoever. One Day he addressed her in
these Terms: I am going to leave you, dear *Zelide*,
said he; my Dear, I am going to leave you. My
Country claims my Arm, but my Heart is yours.
Zelide turn'd pale, and that Instant was the Epoch
of her Misery. She could not speak one Word; but
a tender Sigh was the Forerunner of her Tears.
You are so wise, continued *Hali*, that I do not fear
you will be any Obstacle to me in the Way that
leads to Honour. The more Laurels I shall be
crown'd with, the more I shall be worthy of enjoying you. When I shall have conquer'd our Enemies, I will present you with the same Hand that
obtain'd the Victory, and that can receive its Happiness from none but you. Take that Hand as a
Token of my Love. After these Words he embraced her.

At this Instant enter'd the Father of *Zelide*, who,
full of Confusion and Pensiveness, retired to her A-
partment; where, in the room of somniferous Poppies, Alarm and Disquiet sow'd corroding Cares and
dreadful Anxieties. That beautiful Colour which
shone in her Countenance gave way to Paleness, and
her plump Habit began to diminish. She seem'd
as if she was wasted by a slow Fever, which would
insensibly bring her to her Grave. The fatal Hour
was come, and the Departure of the military Officers was publickly declared by the Sound of a Trum-
pet. Farewel, dear *Hali*, cried the disconsolate Lo-

ver:

ver: My Heart is to undergo more dangerous Combats than those to which you are going to expose yourself. Remember *Zelide*; she swears to be for ever faithful to you. *Hali* departs, and abandons his Lover, who is ready to give up the Ghost. He triumphs over himself, but never did any Triumph cost him so much. In a short Time he arrived before the Enemy's Camp, and a Battle ensued. Animated with the Hopes of seeing again his lovely Fair, he carried Slaughter, Terror, and Death wherever he went. He could not pass one Day without fighting; for he look'd upon every Moment that retarded his Return, as Time of which he wrong'd *Zelide*. With a Handful of Men he attack'd a large Army, and, after having given amazing Proofs of his Valour, he was overpower'd by the Number of his Enemies, who surrounded him on every Side. His Death was inevitable, as well as the Death of all those that were with him. He made new Attempts to save himself, but to no purpose; for he fell down, and a *Tartar* pierced his Heart with a Dagger.

THE Daughter of the Sangiac had Intimation of this fatal Accident by frightful Dreams, which redoubled both her Grief and Anxiety. Though her Father used a great deal of Precaution in telling her this melancholy News, she tore her Veil, and fell into a lethargic Consumption. I was sent for, in order to give her some Relief. By my Care I preserved her Life (if it be Life to pass one's Time in Grief and Pain). I order'd her to take the Country Air, to dispel her Anxiety: But the Arrow that had

pierced

pierced her followed her wherever she went, and with all my Skill I never could cure the Wound of her Heart. She kept out of all Company, and applied herself wholly to the Study of Philosophy: But such Exercise, far from repairing her Strength, was the Way to render her lean. Though she seem'd to be somewhat easy, yet the Remembrance of her dear Lover was still fresh in her Mind, and was the principal Object of her Thoughts. The last Time I saw her she was so thin and lean, that she resembled one of those Spectres whose Bones have nothing to cover them but the Skin. Her Hair, that was fair, became black; and her hollow sparkling Eyes were like those Lights that shine by Night at a great Distance.

I AM very much affected with the Fate of *Zelide*, replied the tender-hearted Odalike. I understand very well, that Love, Grief, and all the other Passions, as well as Study, may render us lean: But by what means can the Passions be destroy'd? Can a Person be insensible? Perhaps, *Abdeker*, you may see the Day when the Charms of *Fatima* will fade. Oh! answer'd the Doctor, if there be any Mortal on Earth so happy as to move your Affection, may it be he whose Soul you are, who lives and breathes by you, and who —— Have a care, cried *Fatima* interrupting the Doctor, (whose Transports were too lively) have a care; the *Kiflar-Agafi* * is at the Door, and perhaps listens to our Discourse. You will im•

* *Kiflar-Agafi* is as much as to say, the *Guardian of the Virgins*, or the *Intendant of the Chambers of the Women*.

mediately

mediately lose your Life, if that Eunuch puts any Suspicion into *Mahomet*'s Head concerning our Conduct. Let us return to *Zelide*, and let us suppose that her Leanness was not the Effect of her Passions, but that she had conquer'd them by a superior Strength, which is not granted to every one. What Method would you take in this Case to restore her to her former Condition, wherein she appeared so agreeable to the Eye. *Fatima*, says *Abdeker*, you propose a Subject whose Explication requires a vast Extent of Knowledge: I expect that your Wit will supply the Defect of what I shall forget to tell you. I shall, in the first Place, enquire into the Cause which hinders the Blood from receiving a sufficient Quantity of nourishing Particles. Secondly, I will endeavour to shew how it may retain the Nourishment it has already acquired. I say in the first Place, that it is necessary to know the Reason why the Blood does not receive a sufficient Quantity of Nourishment; because it would be acting like a blind Man, and a mere chimerical Fancy, to endeavour to remove a Cause that does not exist.

The Want of balsamic Particles in the Blood may proceed either from the Fault of Digestion, or from the Fault of the Diet. The Fault of Digestion is of great Extent, and requires great Penetration and Attention to follow it through all its Progress. In the first Place, bad Digestion may proceed from the Mouth; which happens when the Food is not well chew'd, or when the Spittle is of a bad Quality: This is the Cause that makes old People lean. Secondly, Digestion may be ill perform'd in the Stomach;

mach; which Defect may proceed either from the Stomach's being incapable of Action, or from the bad Quality of its Juices, or the Badness of our Food. This Diforder of the Stomach is commonly accompanied with a Diarrhœa, which weakens the rest of the Body, and wastes it insensibly. If the third Digestion, which is made in the Inteftines, be bad, (which may proceed from several Caufes) the Chyle it forms is fo thick that it cannot pafs into the Blood, or, if it does pafs, it carries along with it the Seeds of infinite Diforders. I shall not mention a Multitude of Obftacles that oppofe the Chyle in its Paffage; for it would lead me to a vaft Number of difficult Queftions, which a Difciple of *Æfculapius* should examine only in his Clofet, that upon every Occafion he may have efficacious Means to obviate them.

The bad Quality of the Diet may produce the fame Effects. The Air that we breathe, if it be too hot or too dry, bad Food, an immoderate Ufe of fpirituous Liquors, too violent Exercife, watching too long, certain Excretions either augmented or fuppreffed, are fo many Caufes that diminifh Fatnefs, and which should excite the Attention of a Phyfician, when the Bufinefs is to repair the Lofs of that Oil which fill'd the Cells of the Adipofe Membrane. Have we fatisfied all thefe Intentions? In general we have; but the moft difficult remains untouch'd. It confifts in retaining in the Blood the balfamic Parts, which should produce in the Body that Kind of Fatnefs which renders it fo agreeable. To this End we should begin to allay the Heat and

Acrimony

Acrimony of the Humours, moderate the Circulation of the Blood, and render the Fibres more elastic
and flexible. I would therefore advise the Patient
to take absorbent Draughts, and use Food that contains a great Quantity of Mucilage. Milk, Eggs,
Jellies, the Flesh of young Animals, and Rice Gruel,
will satisfy a Part of this Intention. I would advise
him likewise to sleep longer than usual, to take no
more Exercise than what is necessary for preserving
his Strength, and to endeavour to keep his Mind
easy and undisturb'd. Frequent Bathing will also
be very efficacious.

I BELIEVE, replied the beautiful Odalike, that
your last Prescription is excellent. I remember when
I lived at *Cotatis* *, in the House of *Kara-Isouf*, to
have seen one of those *Egyptian* Women, who follow no other Occupation but that of fattening the
Ladies. She told me of Baths, and the Manner of
using them. I will give you a brief Account of
what she said upon that Subject, that you may let
me know your Opinion thereof.

As the *Egyptians*, said she, live under a very
warm Climate, they have more need than other Na-
tions to bathe often, in order to wash away the Sweat
and Dust that adheres to their Skin. For this Purpose they have publick Bathing-Houses; to which
the Women resort in Crouds, not only with a Design to keep themselves clean, but also to render
themselves more agreeable; for the Men of this
Country love Women mostly on account of their

* The Capital of *Georgia*.

Fatness,

Fatness. For this Reason their chief Study is to make themselves fat; which some of them do to such a prodigious Degree, that they can hardly move themselves, so that they are always confined to their Bed. In order to acquire this Degree of Fatness, they bathe themselves several Days successively in lukewarm Water. They stay so long in these Baths that they eat and drink therein. That *Egyptian* Woman told me, that she herself grew fat in a very short Time by this Method. During the Time they are in the Bath they take every half Hour some Broth made of a fat Pullet, and stuffed with sweet Almonds, Hasel-Nuts, Dates, and Pistachio-Nuts. After taking this Sort of Broth four times, they eat a fat Pullet entirely, all but the Head. When they come out of the Bath, they are rubb'd over with Perfumes and sweet-scented Pomatums; and after that some of them take Myrobalans * before they go to Bed; others take a Draught prepared with Gum Tragacanth and Sugar-candy.

THIS Practice, says *Abdeker*, is conformable to the Principles I have laid down. The Woman did not impose upon you, for that Method is much practised in *Cairo*; and I am sure it would have a more speedy and constant Success in Countries that are not so hot and dry as *Egypt*.

* There are several Sorts of this Fruit; some are black, others of an Orange-Colour; some are round, others oblong. The *Arabians* first made use of them in Medicine.

CHAP.

C H A P. XIII.

Of particular L E A N N E S S.

THE Subject of our present Discourse, continued the Doctor, shall be the Leanness of certain Parts of the Body.   The Hands, the Breast, the
Thighs, may be quite void of Flesh, whilst the Face
is as plump as ever: But the general Method I have
proposed should be applied to all particular Cases.
It is said that the Emperor *Germanicus,* whose Thighs
were very lean, and who had thereupon consulted
all the Physicians of the Age he lived in, was cured
of that Defect by riding after his Meals.   There
are some Cases wherein the Doctor should abandon
the Cure, and the Patient should trust entirely to
the Strength of Nature.   When any Part of the
Body becomes lean and wither'd either by a Wound
or by the Palsy, it can never be restored to its former Vigor, by all the Succours that Art can furnish.
However, we should not for this Reason conclude, that
Medicine is altogether inefficacious and useless.   No
body was ever so injudicious as to accuse a Physician
of Ignorance, for not being able to make a Mem-
ber grow in the Place of one that was cut off.

I AM not tired of listening to you, replied *Fatima.*   It is the Desire I have of learning Things that
are of great Use and Consequence, which has made
me give you so much Trouble.   My Attention has
been so taken up with the Subject you have treated

of,

of, that I quite forgot that *Mahomet* was to appear in the Divan *, and that he will not fail to pay me a Visit. Farewel, *Abdeker*; endeavour to gain the Confidence of *Haflaler Agafi*. I expect you will come to me to-morrow, after visiting the Infirmary.

CHAP. XIV.

A Description of MAHOMET.

*A*BDEKER was hardly out of *Fatima's* Apartment, when *Mahomet* enter'd the Divan. *Mahomet* was thick, and of a middle Stature. His Constitution was fit for all Sorts of Fatigue, and his Health never received the least Shock before the Disorder of which the *Arabian* Physician had happily cured him. He was of an Olive-colour'd Complexion, his Eye-brows very thick, and his Eyes were so fierce that he look'd like a Savage. He had such a long Hawk-Nose, that it seem'd to touch his lower Lip: All which render'd his Countenance formidable; but he made it still more so by cruel and bloody Actions. He was more ambitious than *Alexander*, and a greater Warriour than *Cæsar*. He was endow'd with the most opposite Qualities: Sweetness and Anger, Humanity and Cruelty, appear'd alternately in his Actions. His Virtues for the most part proceeded from Reflection or from Policy, and his Vices were always the Effect of his Temper,

---

* The Privy Council.

      The

The firſt time he ſaw *Fatima*, an involuntary Con-
fuſion ſeized all his Senſes. His Heart, which never before experienced any thing but the impetuous
Flames that were kindled in his Veins by the hot
and vigorous Quality of his Blood, at that Inſtant
began to feel the raviſhing Sweetneſs of a chaſte
Paſſion. Accuſtom'd to the Operations of War, he
beſieged a Heart after the ſame Manner that he
block'd up a Garriſon. Seldom meeting with Re-
ſiſtance, he was a bold daring Soldier; and always
crown'd with Victory, he ſaw his Enemies kiſs his
Footſteps, and tremble at the Sound of his Name.
Uſing his Wives like Slaves, Majeſty ſat by his Side
during the Time it was to yield up its Place to
Pleaſure.

FATIMA in an Inſtant could chain that Lion
which ſeem'd ſo untameable, and that Maſter who
gave Fetters to all *Aſia*. Seized with Awe at the
Sight of *Fatima*, as if ſhe was ſome Goddeſs, he approach'd her with downcaſt Eyes, and threw himſelf at her Feet. I conquer Men, ſaid he, who ſerve
me out of Fear; and you ſubdue Hearts, which you
enchain with Love. Reign over me, and all my
Court and Empire ſhall ſhew you their Submiſſion.
Let me but reign in your Soul, and I ſhall think my-
ſelf Monarch of the Univerſe. *Fatima*, who had
been only accuſtom'd to a ſimple Way of Life, and
to ſuch Diverſions as are common to young Women
of her Age, was aſtoniſh'd and confounded at the
great Honour that was offer'd her. Baſhfulneſs
obliged her to keep Silence for ſome time; but at
length ſhe ſpoke as follows with the utmoſt Modeſty.

Mighty

Mighty Prince, I am sensible of the Value of what you propose me; nor could any thing but your Generosity overlook the vast Disproportion there is between your Rank and mine. Love, replied the Emperor, admits of no Conditions; and there is no Man has so much Reason to doubt whether he is belov'd upon his own Account, as he who is invested with supreme Power. Perhaps we do not love a Person that raises us from nothing merely for his own sake, but on account of the Service he has done us. The Sentiments we have for him are rather those of Gratitude than Love. Reign over my Empire, and command in this Palace, that every one may hasten to pay you his Court, and that all may obey your Laws.

THEY pass'd the rest of the Day over the most splendid Entertainment. *Mahomet*, neglecting for some time the Care of his Empire, order'd Balls, Feasts, Concerts of Musick, and every thing that could amuse the Object of his Love. Like *Hercules* at the Feet of *Omphale*, he thought of nothing but spending his Days in Ease and Luxury.

AFTER *Mahomet* had given *Fatima*, in the Presence of all his Court, the most sincere Marks of his Love, she was conducted to the Apartment appointed for her. There she received the Compliments of her Rivals, whose Curiosity made them very desirous of seeing the Beauty that was so much talk'd of in the Seraglio. Some of them affirm'd she was worthy of the Handkerchief; but others, less judicious or more jealous, found many Faults in her that she had not. *Irene*, the Sultan's Favourite, resolved to secure his

Heart

Heart for herself alone; and in order thereto she took a Step that was beneath her Dignity, but her Interest got the better of her Vanity. She went to visit the young Odalike, and to pay her Compliments to her on account of her great Beauty. After giving her the highest Praises, and preparing her Mind by a very flattering insinuating Discourse, she took her aside, and spoke to her in this Manner. I know the great Affection the Emperor has for you; he loved me with a more violent Passion, but he never loved me so tenderly, or with so much Delicacy. I am not so unjust as to upbraid you with it as a Crime; for that would be insulting the Gods, who were pleased to make you so beautiful. Notwithstanding all this, can I see myself despised at present, without shewing my Dissatisfaction, and bemoaning my Misfortune? In vain did I take so much Pains to gain the Sultan, appeasing his Rage by my obliging Behaviour, mollifying his haughty Humour by my Patience, and fixing his variable Disposition by my Constancy. One Glance of your Eyes had Power enough to overthrow all my innocent Projects, and deprive me of a Hero whom I love notwithstanding all his Failings. I know you artfully refused to quench his Flame. Perhaps it was a Prejudice you might have from your Infancy, or the Bashfulness of a noble Soul, that caused you to delay the Moment that *Mahomet* impatiently longs for, and which he will soon bring about. That is the fatal Moment which *Irene* dreads, since it will be the unhappy Instant that will deprive her of her Lover; and which perhaps *Fatima* wishes for with Impatience,

tience, since it will be the Epoch from whence she
is to begin to share the Honours of a Throne with
the greatest Conqueror in the Universe. Chear up,
dear Odalike, the Heart of a despairing Lover.
Will you be the Cause of *Irene*'s Misery and Death,
by endeavouring to seduce her Lover, and yielding
yourself up to gratify his burning Passion? Tell me;
what have I to hope, or what have I to fear?

I KNOW not, my dear Sultanefs, whether I shall
be guilty of Indiscretion in revealing my Mind to
you, or whether you will believe my Words are sincere and deserve Credit. I assure you I did not seek
the Honours that are intended for me, and that I
could see myself deprived of them without the least
Concern; and as the Emperor's Love does not at all
affect me, the Loss of them would make but little
Impression upon me. His Bounty has confounded
me, but not gain'd my Heart; and his Indifference
would give me less Alarm than his Love.

THE Sultanefs seem'd to be very well satisfied with
this Answer; and as she was going away she embraced *Fatima*, telling her she might depend upon
her Friendship. Whilst this Intrigue was carrying
on in the Seraglio, *Mahomet* studied new Schemes to
please *Fatima*, and to subdue her Soul, which seem'd
insensible to the Offers of his Love. This Disre-
gard, like a Sting, increased his Passion; and the
more, as he expected no Opposition. He order'd a
new Palace to be built, call'd *Geni Serai*, wherein
he might display all his Grandeur and Magnificence,
by the vast Extent of the Building, the Richness and
Splendor of its Furniture, and the Beauty of its

F 3 Gardens.

Gardens. To accomplish his Design, he call'd home
Pacha *Ibrahim*, a very sensible Man, and much at-
tach'd to the Despoine * *Mary*, the Emperor's Mother-in-Law. This Pacha carried on the Work with
so much Expedition, that in a short Time it was fit
for the Reception of *Fatima* and the whole Court.
It was after his Recovery that *Mahomet* first enter'd
this Palace; at which Time he paid the *Georgian*
Lady but a very short Visit, on account of many
Affairs of the greatest Importance that were neglected during his Illness, upon the Dispatch whereof
the Interest of the Empire much depended. It was
about these Affairs that *Mahomet* went to the Divan,
which he did rather out of Policy and Formality,
than with a Design of consulting the Vizirs, and
that he might not be look'd upon as the only Author
of those unhappy Consequences that might attend
some of his rash Undertakings.

AFTER conferring with his Vizirs, he concluded
that War should be declared against *Scanderbeg*.
When he came out of the Divan, he went to see *Fatima*, as she expected, and accosted her in these
Terms. You are the principal Ornament of my Empire; this stately Building that I have erected for
you, and which is a manifest Sign of my Grandeur,
would be an obscure Retreat if you were not present
to enlighten it. It is not without great Reluctance,
and doing Violence to my own Inclination, that I
must leave you for some time; but I will only go
and shew my Troops the Enemy they are to attack,

* A Title that is given to the *Grecian* Princesses.

and

and immediately return and throw myself at your
Feet. *Fatima*, who did not love the Sultan so much
as *Abdeker*, for whom she was consumed by a hidden Flame, answer'd him in Terms that shew'd her
Artfulness and Policy more than her Affection. Great
Sultan, I will not oppose you in any thing that may
tend to your Glory and Renown; for Disgrace would
equally fall upon the Person who is the Cause of it,
and upon him that is its Subject. Take special Care,
however, to preserve a Life so precious to your Empire, and which all your People lately fear'd was at
an End, when it was prolong'd by the Skill of the
learned *Abdeker*. She trembled at pronouncing the
Name of *Abdeker*, whom she loved most dearly; fearing lest the Emperor should suspect she had the Doctor's Interest too much at heart: But the Sultan interpreted her trembling in his own Favour, believing
it proceeded from the Sensibility of his Mistress, and
the Love that she had for him. Flatter'd with this
seeming Proof of her Tenderness, he pass'd the
greatest Part of the Night with her, and entertain'd
her all the time with the most insinuating and courteous Expressions that a Lover could invent. This
Night he found himself in a happy State of Recovery, but nevertheless he contented himself with
passing the Time in admiring his Mistress for her
generous Acknowledgment of his Favours. During
this Time the young Odalike employ'd all the Art,
all the Devices she could think of, in order to prevent the Design of the Sultan consider'd as a passionate Lover, without displeasing him; or as a
despotic

defpotic Prince and Mafter, without provoking him to Rage and Violence *.

C H A P. XV.

Of the Siege of CROYE.

MAHOMET fet out the next Day at the Head of ten thoufand Men. He encamp'd before *Croye*, a City of *Albania*, and Capital of the Dominions of *Scanderbeg*. This City ftands upon a fteep Rock; the Advantages of which Situation, together with the Help of Art, render'd it impregnable, according to the Opinion of moft People, unlefs it were taken by Famine. *Mahomet* befieged it once before under the Command of his Father *Amurat*; but it was defended with fo much Bravery and Conduct, that the *Ottomans* were obliged to raife the Siege, af-

---

* Such Oppofition to the Defires of a Sovereign, who admits no Law but his Will, is furprifing to me, and will undoubtedly furprife the Reader: However, his Hiftory affords us another memorable Example of the fame Nature. When *Mahomet*, in the Year 1470, render'd himfelf Mafter of the City of *Negro-pont*, he made *Paul Erizo*, the *Venetian* Governor, Prifoner. He was a Man of extraordinary Courage and Bravery; and he had a Daughter named *Anne Erizo*, who was alfo one of the Captives. As fhe was a fuperior Beauty, the Janizaries prefented her to the Sultan, who very gladly received fo valuable a Jewel. But never could *Mahomet* prevail over the Virtue of this generous Lady, who chofe to die rather than gratify the Defires of an Enemy, who, after breaking his Word, had inhumanly put her Father to Death.

ter

ter losing the most considerable Part of their Army. *Amurat* laid this so much to heart, that he fell sick and died, not being able to bear the Disgrace of an unsuccessful Expedition.

SCANDERBEG was an Enemy that the *Turkish* Emperor was once more to engage; a formidable Enemy, who cut out more Work for *Mahomet* by his Courage and good Conduct, than all the ill-concerted Leagues of the *European* Princes. No Man knew so well as the King of *Albania* how to turn to Advantage the Situation and Nature of a Country that was full of Woods, Mountains, and Defiles. He continually harrass'd and destroy'd his Enemy by sudden and prudent Sallies, or by artful and well-contrived Ambuscades. One while, like a hasty and impetuous Torrent, he bore down every thing that came in his way: At other times, like Lightning, he penetrated into Places that seem'd to be in the greatest Safety. In a plain open Country he was not able to face the numerous Army of the *Turks*; but, like a skilful General, he had Recourse to Stratagem, by which means he spared the Lives of his Soldiers, defended the Liberty of his Country, and oppofed an impregnable Fortress to the Ambition of the *Ottoman* Emperor.

THE Army being encamp'd before *Croye*, *Mahomet* according to his Custom visited the Out-works, and summon'd the Governor to surrender. The Garrison answer'd the Chamade with Flights of Arrows and a Discharge of Fire-Arms. This Volley was succeeded by a sudden and most vigorous Sally, by which great Part of the *Turks* were kill'd. *Mahomet*

met on his Side push'd on the Siege with the utmost
Vigour; but the brave Defence made by the Be-
sieged, and the various Stratagems of their General,
gave him to understand, that having an Enemy of
so much Courage and Conduct to deal with, the
Conquest of *Albania* would cost him above a Year.
Besides, the Image of *Fatima* was often present to
his Imagination; he burn'd with the Desire of seeing her once more, and of triumphing over her
Heart. The Love of Glory still detain'd him; but
the Love of *Fatima*, much more powerful, hurried
him away whether he would or no. He preferr'd
the Myrtle-Wreath to the Laurel-Crown, and left
the Command of his Army to *Mustapha* and *Ballabanus*, who was the first that enter'd Sword in Hand
into *Constantinople*. These two Generals were order'd to block up the City of *Croye*; and having
given this Order, *Mahomet* return'd with the utmost
Expedition to his Seraglio.

C H A P. XVI.

Of Baths, *and the* Whiteness *of the* Skin.

DURING the Absence of the Emperor, *Abdeker* paid frequent Visits to *Fatima*, whom he
loved every Day more and more. The young Odalike, in order to furnish a Pretext for his Visits, and
to prevent the Suspicions that her Inspectors might

entertain

entertain of her Conduct, pretended to be slightly
indisposed. Upon this her Doctor order'd to use the
Baths, and to take a Dose of Serquis *.

THE Baths were the most magnificent Buildings in
Constantinople. Those that went to bathe were led
first into a Porch paved with the finest Marble, en-
rich'd with a most curious Piece of Mosaic Work.
From thence they were conducted into a Chamber
quite surrounded with Sofas, to repose themselves
upon before they went into the Bath. After un-
dressing in this Chamber, they enter'd the Bathing-
Room, which was adorn'd with six Columns of Jas-
per, that sustain'd a Cupola glazed all over. The
Walls were all incrusted with Mother of Pearl, which
on every Side caused such a Reflection of the Light
upon a Person in the Bath, that it gave the Skin a
Lustre which made it look more white and smooth
than usual. The Bathing-Place was in the Middle
of the Room, in the Form of a Shell, and was sup-
ported by a Kind of Throne adorn'd with Coral,
and with the most scarce and valuable Shells and
Pearls that could be procured. The Use of this
Throne was to hide the Pipes, some of which furnish'd warm Water, and others cold; so that *Fatima*
could give her Bath any Degree of Heat she pleased.
On one Side of this Hall there were great Caul-
drons, wherein were boil'd aromatic Plants, whose
Vapours were so artificially convey'd to all Parts of
the Hall, that they caused not only a gentle Heat,
but also a most agreeable Smell. The like Work,

* See OBSERVATION II.

which

which was on the oppofite Side of the Hall, was cover'd with rich Carpets.   Under a Canopy adorn'd
with precious Stones, which dazzled the Eyes of the
Beholders, there was a Bed of the fofteft Down;
and about this Bed there were Pans of Gold, wherein were burnt the fweeteft Perfumes that the Eaft
could afford.   At this Place *Fatima*, as fhe came out
of the Bath, was waited upon by a great many Women that were employ'd for that Purpofe, who wiped
her Body, and rubb'd her with the moft fragrant
Spices.   Here fhe was to take fome Hours Repofe,
after being perfumed with the moft fweet-fcented
Odours.

A B D E K E R coming to the Door of this delightful Place, *Hammangi Bachi* was at a ftand whether
he fhould let him in, no Man being permitted to enter there but the Emperor.   But *Abdeker* having informed him that *Fatima* was indifpofed and wanted
his Affiftance, and that he would take a bad Method to gain *Mahomet*'s Favour, if he fhould be the
Caufe of prolonging the Illnefs of his darling Object; at this *Hammangi* open'd the Door, and *Abdeker* came to the very Place where the *Georgian* Lady
was in the Bath.   The naked Graces of *Fatima*, cover'd only with a Veil of cryftal Water, fix'd all his
Attention.   His Heart fwam in Pleafure, and his
Eyes were enliven'd with Delight, but his Mouth
was clofed by the Prefence of the Women that attended their Miftrefs.

F A T I M A, at the Sight of *Abdeker*, burn'd in the
midft of the Water.   The Satisfaction that appear'd
in her Countenance feem'd to correfpond with his
Defires.

Defires. Affecting one while to change her Situa-ation, fhe uncover'd thofe Treafures, the Poffeffion whereof the Doctor would have preferr'd to the greateft Happinefs on Earth. Another while, rifing above the Surface of the Water, fhe fhew'd a Bofom that feem'd to invite his Kiffes. The two Lovers equally inflamed each other, and *Fatima* began to repent that fhe had fent for her Phyfician, who could hardly fetch Breath, and whofe Extafy of Pleafure which he felt at firft was now become the greateft Torment. A critical Moment this, wherein it was neceffary for *Abdeker* to employ all his Prudence and Refolution to be Mafter of himfelf! He endeavour'd to divert his Thoughts another way, and to banifh the lively Ideas he had form'd, at the fame time that his Senfes were moft agreeably flatter'd.

IT is time, faid he to *Fatima*, to take a Bowl of Serquis: The Bath has fufficiently open'd your Pores, and Perfpiration will be free and copious. Immedi-ately *Chryfolite* *, who was the Girl in whom *Fatima* had the greateft Confidence, brought a Bowl that was made of a fingle Agate. *Abdeker* had the Pleafure to fill the Cup with Serquis, and prefent it to the charming Odalike, who thank'd him very courte-oufly, affuring him fhe never before found that Li-quor fo delicious, and that Remedies received from fo valuable a Hand could not fail of producing fa-lutary Effects. I have this Day taken the Place of the Cup-bearer of the Gods, replied *Abdeker*; I wifh I could, after his Example, pour Immortality into

---

* This is the Name of a precious Stone of a golden Colour.

G   your

your Cup. Their Converfation now became very ferious; but fortunately there was none prefent but *Chryfolite*, and fome Dwarfs that were both deaf and dumb. It was dangerous, however, to continue talking in the fame Strain. Several Women, who were in the neighbouring Chambers, might hear them, and imagine that fuch affectionate Language did not proceed from the Emperor's Orders. *Abdeker* was very fenfible of this, notwithftanding the Tranfports of Love wherewith he was feized. He therefore refolved, for the greater Security of the lovely *Georgian* Lady, to fpeak only of fuch Things as could give no Sufpicion, and fuch as were the Subject of their former Converfation.

You are, faid he, fo excellent a Mirrour of Beauty, that one cannot look at you without reflecting upon a charming Face and Shape, and without defiring to preferve them when prefent, or to recover them when abfent. You granted me, that there are Means to repair the Damage that too much Fatnefs or too much Leannefs can do to Beauty. I am now going to fpeak of a Thing that is the more effential to our Subject, as it is the firft that makes an Impreffion upon the Eye. It is the Colour of the Skin, (as you may eafily guefs) which when it is pale, yellow, brown, blackifh, purple, is difagreeable to the Eye, becaufe fuch Colours fuppofe a particular Diftemper in the Subject. This indeed does not relate to the *Ethiopians*, who believe that a true black Skin and a flat Nofe are effential to Beauty. I only fpeak here of the Opinion received in our own Climate, where we reckon a white Skin, whofe Surface is

fpread

spread over with the Colour of Roses, to be the most perfect and the most agreeable, as to what regards its Colour. This Opinion seems to be founded upon Reason, since we find that such a Colour denotes a good Constitution, and that it always changes when Health is impair'd. The Colour of the Skin is the characteristic Sign whereby we distinguish the different Constitutions of Mankind. It is by this Sign, for Example, we distinguish a bilious from a sanguine Constitution, and a phlegmatic from a melancholic Temperament. Those that are of a sanguine Constitution have commonly the most lively and the most beautiful Colour. It is just that such a Complexion should receive from the Hands of Nature the greatest Gifts of Beauty, since it has the greatest Efficacy to excite Men and Women to amorous Pleasures.

ABDEKER, replied *Fatima*, am I of that Complexion? I suppose it is out of Complaisance you praise it so much. But I have heard from Men of good Understanding, that People of such a Constitution are lascivious, inconstant, very hasty and passionate. I own, answer'd the Doctor, that what you have said is in some measure true: As for your Part, you have all the Virtues of that Constitution without its Faults; your Body contains all its good Qualities, and your Soul is of the Temper of the Prudent. I find, replied *Fatima*, you know how to extricate yourself out of a Difficulty. However, I have some Objections to make you; but proceed.

THERE are several internal Causes, continued the Doctor, that may change the white and vermilion

Colour of which I am speaking; as, for Instance, a Disorder of the Stomach, Obstructions of the Liver, a Suppression of the monthly Evacuations, and many other Causes, which, by giving fatal Strokes to the Health, at the same time insult and injure Beauty. But you will be pleased to excuse my not making mention of the Cure of such Ailments; for that could not be done without penetrating into the most hidden and profound Secrets of Medicine. I only promised to walk along with you in the Gardens, not in the inward Sanctuaries of this Science.

The exterior Causes are the Food which we commonly take: The Air also has a singular Power either to nourish or wither the Lilies and Roses of a fair Complexion. Hence it is, that such as inhabit temperate Climates are fair and of a good Colour. Hence also we find the Reason, why those who expose themselves too much to the Heat of the Sun are of a tawny Colour. Too much Watching, hard Labour, as well as too much Sleep, spoil the Colour of the Skin. Sadness, Fear, too much Application to Study, Remorse of Conscience, Excess of carnal Pleasures, produce the same Effect. Love, that should protect those who adore him by their good Wishes, but fail to pay him their Tribute either out of Prejudice or some other strong Motive, has sometimes the Cruelty to cast a Blemish on their Countenance, which cannot be effaced otherwise than by the Remedy they have neglected. It is thus that many young Girls contract either the Green Sickness or the Jaundice, for having refused Love the Sacrifice that he required of them.

At

At these Words *Fatima* look'd at *Chrysolite*, in whose Face one might still discern Features of an exquisite Beauty; but her Cheeks were bloated, her Eye-lids swoln, her Skin somewhat yellow, and she had a livid Circle about her Eyes. I believe, said the young Odalike, that *Chrysolite* belongs to the Class of young Women you are speaking of, and wants your Advice. The Remedies you prescribe seem to me as pleasing to the Taste, as they are efficacious in curing Distempers.

CHRYSOLITE, who had no Suspicion of becoming the Subject of their Discourse, blush'd. She was fully satisfied of the Truth of what was spoken, but her Soul was in such Agitation, that she could think of no better Means to avoid the Questions of *Abdeker* and the Looks of *Fatima*, than to slip away between two Curtains, which she could not effect without discovering her Confusion.

A BAD Choice of Food, continued *Abdeker*, and Surfeits occasion'd by eating or drinking to Excess, are to be reckon'd among the Causes that injure the Colour of the Skin. They say that such as make use of Barley-Bread are paler than those who eat * Mays-Bread. It is said also, that Cummin and Bishop's-Weed destroy the Complexion, by a Property peculiar to those Plants. It was by such Means that the Disciples of *Porcius Latro* imitated the excessive Paleness of that Orator. It was by the same Means also that *Julius Vindex* deceived the Emperor *Nero*, in counterfeiting Sickness. As Salt Meat and

* *Turkish* or *Indian* Wheat.

Hung

Hung Beef are apt to produce thick Humours, the
Use of them is very capable of deftroying the Graces
of a beautiful Complexion. A continued Ufe of
muddy Water, that has a bad Quality, produces the
fame Effect. I remember to have read, that when
our Forefathers wanted to know whether the Waters
of certain Countries were good, they made it their
Bufinefs to examine the Complexion of the Inhabitants. If all the natural Secretions and Excretions
of the Body be not duly perform'd, the Skin will
not have the lively handfome Colour I am fpeaking
of. We may find out, by giving the leaft Attention
to what paffes before our Eyes, that there is no Man
but carries in his Face the Marks that denote whether he is too lax or too coftive, or whether the Fil-
tration or Circulation of certain Humours be interrupted. I fhall treat of each of thefe Caufes in particular, that I may have an Opportunity of giving
you a full Account of the Remedies that are proper
in each Circumftance.

THE Deformities of the Skin are in Proportion to
the Temperature of the Air: Therefore we ought
carefully to fhun the Air that is too hot or too cold;
and confequently we fhould avoid the frozen Northern Winds, and the tempeftuous Gales of the South.
The Ancients, when they fold any Slaves, (as they
do in the *Bazar* *) cover'd their Faces with a Kind
of Mud which is found in the Troughs of thofe who
grind Iron or Steel Inftruments, to preferve them
from the too fharp Impreffions of the Air. I have

---

* A Market in *Conftantinople*, where Slaves are fold.

been

been aſſured that the Inhabitants of *Genoa* rub their
Faces with the Juice of Morel *, whenever they are
obliged to expoſe themſelves to the Heat of the Sun:
But I know nothing ſo good for keeping the Face
from being tann'd, as the Veil uſed in this Country.
However, if in ſpite of theſe Precautions the Skin
becomes wither'd, the diſtill'd Waters of Roſes,
Flower-de-Luce, Strawberries, Beans, Melons, Bur-
net, Aſſes Milk, Women's Milk, and ſeveral other
cooling and emollient Remedies, may be uſed with
much Succeſs. I know ſome Women who are particularly careful of their Beauty: They aſſure me
that nothing whitens the Skin ſo much as to take
the Air in a calm Night, and to walk by the Water
ſide in the Time of a Fog. I ſhall ſpeak of this
Caſe more at large, when I come to treat of Freckles. In the mean time I will give you an Account
of an Affair that is very ſuitable to our preſent Subject.

A YOUNG *Turkiſh* Girl, whoſe Name was *Zinzima*, was Slave to *Azor*, Kadileſquer † of *Erzerum*:
She was the Daughter of a Boſtangi ‡ of *Conſtantinople*. *Azor* employ'd her in cultivating the Plants
of his Kitchen-Garden, and would ſometimes mark
out a Taſk for her himſelf. *Zinzima* had a brown
and lively Eye, a well-proportion'd Face, but a
tawny Skin. Beſides, ſhe was of a good Stature,
well made, and very nimble and handy in every

---

* This is a Plant that is very emollient, cooling, and nar-
cotic.

† A Judge in *Turky*, like a Chief Juſtice in *England*.

‡ A Gardener of the Seraglio.

thing

thing she undertook. Her Answers were smart and
sensible, and her Discourse was pleasant and entertaining, by reason of her innocent Jokes. The Kadilesquer was a Man of excellent Parts. He lost his
Wife (whom he lov'd very much) six Months before,
upon which he abandon'd his Haram *, gave himself up entirely to Grief, and lived alone in a Country House he had in the Neighbourhood of *Erzerum*. When he quitted the City, he swore that he
would never engage his Heart any more in the
Chains of Love; and that he might the better fulfil
his Oath, he resolved to live in Retirement. At first
he took no manner of Notice of *Zinzima*; but his
Tears drying up by degrees, he view'd her as a most
amiable Object. He thought she would be very
glad, and think herself highly honour'd, if he should
require her to gratify his Passion. Accordingly he
approach'd her with a bold Air, and attack'd her
as a Place that would make no Defence: But *Zinzima*, who had as much Ambition and Dissimulation
in her Heart, as she had Penetration in her Head,
made so stout a Resistance, that she quite wearied the
Kadilesquer in spite of all his Efforts. By this Opposition she thought to increase *Azor*'s Heat and Ea-
gerness; and to turn that Flame, which undoubtedly was kindled by his long Abstinence, into a Passion that might procure her very great Advantages.
Azor, though repulsed, did not drop his Pretensions;
and to accomplish his Design he made use of In-

---

* *Seraglio* is the Place where the Grand Signior keeps his
Concubines. The Apartments wherein the Concubines of private Persons are shut up are call'd *Harams*.

treaties, Threatnings, Prefents, and ill Ufage. *Zin-zima*, however, remain'd inflexible, and all he could do was to no Purpofe. At length the Kadilefquer, defpairing of obtaining his End, afk'd her what Conditions fhe required of him to comply with his Defires. You may be affured, replied *Zinzima*, I will never confent to fatisfy your Paffion till you marry me. I would gladly be your Wife, but not the vile Inftrument of your Pleafure. As foon as ever your Defires were gratified, you would fend me away to your Haram, to increafe the Number of thofe Slaves who tremble at the Name of one Man, who is no more than their Equal.

AZOR fmiled at hearing her Propofal. To be fure, faid he, you forget that you are a Slave, or you forget that you fpeak to a Judge, who makes all tremble before his Tribunal. I know, replied *Zinzima*, that in the *Ottoman* Empire a *Turk* never determines himfelf in marrying a Wife but by his own Choice; nor ever pays any Regard to Birth, which depends upon nothing but mere Chance.

AZOR being very fenfible that he had to deal with a Perfon who could not eafily be overcome by Force, thought it more prudent to furprife her in her Retrenchments, than to attack her openly in Front. Accordingly he made a Propofal to *Zinzima*, which feem'd to him impoffible to be accomplifh'd. I am willing, faid he, to fubmit to your Way of Reafoning, and to raife you from the State of a Slave to be my Wife, but on this Condition, that you change your tawny Colour, and make it as white as Milk, and as bright as Snow.

ANY

Any one but *Zinzima* would have defpair'd at fuch a Propofal, for fhe had naturally a brown Complexion: But fhe did not want for Expedients to furmount all Obftacles. She knew that I came fometimes to vifit her Mafter; and one Day fhe ftopp'd me as I was going to fee him in the Garden. After fome Difcourfe, wherein fhe reprefented the Paffion that *Azor* had for her, and the Love that fhe had for him, fhe told me the Condition upon which her Mafter would agree to marry her. Having reflected a good while on the Method fhe fhould take to obtain her Wifhes, I advifed her to foften her Skin by wafhing it often with Goat's Milk. Some Days after I brought her a Pomatum compofed of the Oil of Ben, Bifmuth, and Wax; to which I gave fince the Name of Paint*. As foon as fhe had fpread this over her Face, fhe became as white as Snow. *Azor* was furprifed at this Change; and as he look'd upon it as a fure Proof of her Love, he ftood to his Promife and married her.

I admire, fays *Fatima*, the Conduct of *Zinzima*; and I am equally furprifed at her Refolution, and at the Method you took to make her Project fucceed. It is not always poffible, replied *Abdeker*, to explain the Conduct of Women: Sometimes it is eafier to dive into the Secrets of Medicine, which appear to you fo myfterious. To render this Phænomenon, which difengaged *Azor* from his Oath, the more durable, I advifed *Zinzima* to obferve as exact a Diet as a Perfon newly recover'd from a Fit of Sicknefs;

* See OBSERVATION III.

for

for whoever is defirous of preferving a beautiful Complexion ought´ to endeavour to generate good Humours, which cannot be obtain'd but by living foberly, and ufing a great deal of Precaution in the Choice of the Food. For this Reafon I order'd her to avoid all Sorts of Food that are hard to be digefted, or that produce bad Juices; and in particular bad Water, bitter Fruits, and fuch as are apt to give the Cholick, and too falt and high-feafon'd Ragouts.

THE Ancients had a certain Prejudice with regard to the Food that fhould be ufed in order to preferve Beauty. They pretended that the Skin became handfomer, and of a better Colour, by eating Hare's Flefh feven Days fucceffively. *Diafcorides* affures us that the Skin receives an additional Luftre and Beauty by eating Chiche-Peafe and dried Figs, and by purging from time to time with Agaric.

SOME Phyficians affert, that Pepper, Cinnamon, Saffron, and Afparagus, contribute in a particular Manner to beautify the Skin; but the Efficacy of thefe Drugs confifts either in ftirring up the Organs of Digeftion when they are too flow in performing their Functions, or in the Property they have of dividing and attenuating the ftagnating Humours.' Hence it is evident, that they naturally fall into that Clafs of Cofmetics, whofe Action depends upon a determin'd Property. We fhould never admit of fpecific Qualities in Drugs that contain no fuch Thing, or that feem to be nothing but occult Properties, which are entirely contrary to found Reafoning. But without entering any farther into thefe Enquiries, I fay it would

would be in vain to take all the neceſſary Precautions I have mention'd, without keeping the Soul in a calm Situation, free from all Paſſion and Anxiety. He that has too eager a Deſire after Learning, grows pale by Study. The Criminal, who expects in a Dungeon the juſt Puniſhment of his Crimes, becomes of the Colour of Lead. The wicked Wretch, whoſe Conſcience is tortured by Remorſe, looks wan and pale. He that ſuffers himſelf to be overwhelm'd by Grief, or conquer'd by Melancholy, has a brown and yellow Complexion. He that abandons himſelf to the Tranſports of Love changes Colour as often as a Dove's Neck. In a Word, there is nothing contributes ſo much to preſerve the beautiful Colour I have been ſpeaking of, as Calmneſs and Tranquillity of Mind.

LASTLY, I adviſe the taking care that the Humours may be ſeparated in a ſufficient Quantity by their proper Filtres, and that the Excrements may paſs in due Proportion through the Ways that Nature has appointed for them.

I AM acquainted with an Iman * who is ſo ſcrupulous in this Point, that he will not wait till Nature of her own accord ſhall perform her ordinary Functions: Every Morning he takes two or three Clyſters to comfort his Bowels, and to keep up a freſh Colour. This Method has ſo well anſwer'd his Intentions, that there is hardly a Man has ſo freſh a Skin as he, or ſo plump and fair a Complexion. One

---

* A *Turkiſh* Eccleſiaſtic, who officiates as a Prieſt in their Devotions at the Moſques.

would

would take his Perfon to be the Seat both of Health and Delicacy. I am perfuaded that Clyfters are very ufeful in this Cafe, and that they greatly contribute to give the Skin a Luftre: But in my Opinion they fhould be adminifter'd with Moderation, left the Ufe of them fhould degenerate into a Habit, as it commonly happens when they are taken to Excefs.

AFTER fo many Obfervations fupported by Reafon and Experience, I fhould have nothing farther to fay, except concerning Baths, which are fo neceffary for keeping the Skin fair, for cleanfing its Impurities, and giving it that Supplenefs of which the Air deprives it by its continual Contact: But you underftand this Subject fo well, as you have fhew'd me in fpeaking of it fo fkilfully, that I think it needlefs to dwell upon it any longer.

WHAT I faid about Baths, replied *Fatima*, was fo fuperficial, that I believe a great deal remains to be added upon that Head. You endeavour in vain, *Abdeker*, to excufe yourfelf from faying any more concerning them. There are feveral Things relating to this Article which I fhould be very glad to know, and I fhall be difpleafed if you deny me that Favour. I was loth to tire you, fays *Abdeker*, with a Repetition of Things that Reafon and Experience have already taught you: But, to pleafe you, I will entertain you with fome particular Cafes, and you muft blame yourfelf if you fhould happen to be weary.

PEOPLE commonly ufe Baths as much for Pleafure, and for keeping themfelves clean, as for the fake of Health. Neverthelefs one ought to take

certain

certain Precautions in order to receive Benefit from them, and to avoid several fatal Consequences that may ensue when they are used imprudently.

Baths produce several good Effects, besides those I have already spoken of. They retard the Motion of the Blood, quench the immoderate Heat of the interior Parts, dilute thick Humours, curb the excessive Agitation and Vivacity of the Spirits, soften the Hardness of the Viscera, asswage violent Pains, open the Pores of the Skin, and occasion a free Circulation. Hence it is plain that Baths cannot be valued too much, since they produce such salutary Effects, from whence Beauty draws such great Advantages: But Bathing, as well as the best of Remedies, when used inconsiderately, occasions the greatest Evils.

We ought not to go into a Bath when the Stomach is too full, because in that Case it diminishes Digestion. A great many have lost their Lives by being so rash as to bathe in such Circumstances. It is also dangerous to enter the Water when the Fibres are not sufficiently elastic, or when the Blood is too thin; when the Humours are in too great a Motion by a Fever, or by some violent Passion; after being over-heated by Exercise, and the Body all in a Sweat. For want of necessary Precautions in these Circumstances, there have often ensued very dangerous and obstinate Distempers, which sometimes open the gloomy Avenues that lead to the Grave.

Several People may receive much Benefit from bathing in River Water; but I am here speaking only of domestic Baths, and advise the Use of them lukewarm,

lukewarm, or in the same Degree of Heat as our Body. Baths that are too hot wither the Skin, consume the Spirits, and take away the Strength. There are other Baths that are called artificial; such, for Example, as contain aromatic Plants, or emollient Herbs. Such Baths have all the Properties of the natural ones, and likewise communicate to the Body an aromatic Essence, which makes it emit a sweet Smell; but the natural Baths are more efficacious for softening the Callosities of the Skin. The *Jews* and *Egyptians* having observed the great Use that Dyers made of *Tincar* *, in order to give a Lustre to Silk, employ'd it also with Success in their Baths, in order to render the Skin more fair. Some amorous Women bathe themselves in Milk, to make their Skin more smooth and delicate, and sometimes with a View of curing it of a troublesome Itching. I I have read in History, that *Poppæa*, the Wife of *Nero*, would bathe herself in nothing but Asses Milk, and that she kept five hundred of those Animals to furnish her a sufficient Quantity of Milk for that Purpose. This Kind of Milk, as well as Goat's Milk, takes away the Wrinkles of the Skin, renders it white, and gives it a certain Gloss that pleases both the Senses of Seeing and Feeling.

BESIDES Baths for the whole Body, there are Half-Baths, as those for bathing the Feet. It is also customary to wash some particular Parts, the Face and Hands for Example, and likewise some other Parts, which otherwise, on account of their

---

* An *Arabian* Word, which signifies *Borax*.

natural

natural Heat by the Quality of the Humours that pass through them, and by reason that they are continually cover'd, would exhale a most disagreeable and stinking Smell, or would be subject to a great many Ailments if one should neglect to wash them, especially in such a warm Climate as this. It was for this Reason that *Mahomet* had the wise Precaution to order the *Musulmans* to wash often; which in my Opinion is rather one of the Laws that relate to the Preservation of Health, than a Precept of Religion, which directs us to purify the Soul by the frequent Use of Externals.

HERE I might display all the Riches of the Toilet, by making a Rehearsal of all the Waters that are prepared to beautify the Skin and give it a handsome Colour, and by enumerating all the Kinds of Paint that have been invented to give a Lustre to the Skin of the Face, and all the Sorts of Paste that are used for washing the Hands: But this Subject is almost inexhaustible; and if we may judge of the Importance of a Thing by the daily Enquiries of Men, and by the prodigious Number of Receipts that we find as well for preserving it, as for recovering it when it is impaired or lost, there never has been any Subject so ample nor so fertile. You will therefore be pleased to excuse me from speaking of it this Day: You have now been a long time in the Bath, and I am even afraid I have occasioned you to exceed the Limits that are usually prescribed by Physicians in such Cases. As for the rest, you have lost nothing; for I see you have an earnest Desire of being instructed in every thing. In a short Time I will

will give you a small Manuscript, wherein I have collected with great Care the Receipts of the best Compositions that have ever been invented for embellishing the Colour of the Skin *.

FATIMA commended *Abdeker*'s Proposal, thank'd him for his Complaisance, and spoke to him as follows: I intreat you, dear *Abdeker*, said she, to be so kind as go directly to the Porch, where you will find *Chrysolite*; ask her some Questions about her Condition, and give great Attention to what she says; do what you can to cure her, and you will oblige me very much. The Doctor went accordingly, after protesting to *Fatima* that he desired nothing more than to oblige her, and that his Art would fail him if he did not find out some efficacious Remedy for *Chrysolite*'s Disorder.

* See Observation IV.

The End *of the* First Part.

Observation I.

IN this Part of the Manuscript there was a Paragraph written in the *Perfian* Language, which the Author forbids the Translation of into the common Tongues. Therefore to satisfy his Intention I thought myself obliged to translate it into *Latin*.

Si mulierum, says he, *finus pudoris fit nimiùm dilatatus, quod accidit tum propter partium flacciditatem, tum propter frequentes coïtus, debent mulieres tunc uti fequentibus remediis.*

Then follows this Receipt.

Take Gall-Nuts, and boil them in Wine with Cloves; dip a Piece of Linen into the Liquor, and apply it to the Part. Or you may use some of the following Drugs: Alum, Vitriol, *Armenian* Bole, Dragon's Blood, Mastich, Sealed Earth, Gum *Arabic*, the Juice of Acacia, Myrrh, &c. Leaves of Plantain, of the Holly-Rose, of the Mastich-tree, of Knot-grass, the Roots of Bistort, Tormentil, of the small and great Comfrey, the Flowers and Fruit of the Pomegranate-tree, Cyprefs-Nuts, Acorns, the Fruit of the Service-tree before it is ripe, Red Roses, &c. Such of the aforesaid Ingredients as you make choice of are to be used in a Decoction made with Red Wine or Vinegar. Dip a Compress
into

into the Decoction, and apply it to the Part. All
thefe Drugs may furnifh Pomatums and diſtill'd Waters, that will have the fame Virtue as their De-
coctions. For Example:

TAKE Oil of bitter Almonds four Ounces, of
white Wax an Ounce; melt both together in a Sand-
Heat; add of burnt Alum two Ounces, and a Dram
of Alkanet. This Mixture, when cold, forms a red
Pomatum. Or,

TAKE Alum, white Vitriol, and green Vitriol, of
each half an Ounce; diffolve them in Plantain and
Knot-grafs Water, of each fix Ounces. Strain the
Liquor for Ufe. This Water is very ſtyptic.

Decoction of Cypreſs-Nuts.

TAKE Cyprefs-Nuts, Gall-Nuts, of each eight
Ounces; the Filings of Steel prepared with Vinegar,
burnt Alum, of each four Ounces; the Medicinal
Stone, the Root of Pomegranate, of each an Ounce
and a half; bruife them together, and mix them according to Art. Boil the Mixture in a fufficient
Quantity of ſtrong Red Wine, or in Plantain-Water.

THIS Decoction may be alfo employ'd with Succefs to bind and make lean fome Parts of the Body
that grow too fat. In fuch Cafes you may dip a
Spunge in the faid Decoction, and after fqueezing it
a little apply it to the Part.

Observation II.

THE Serquis is the *Elichryfum*, or Golden Cud-
weed. It is to be ufed after the manner of
Tea, and is called the *Tea of the Sultanefs*. *Paul
Lucas* brought fome of it into *France*. Its Tafte is
delicious; and, after examining it with Attention, I
found that it refembled very nearly what refults from
a Spoonful of Spirituous Vulnerary Water mix'd with
two Spoonfuls of River-Water.

THE Virtue of this Plant is wonderful. It pre-
ferves the Complexion fo frefh and fair, that a Woman of Seventy after ufing it will look as if fhe was
not above Thirty-five. It grows at the Foot of a
Mountain near *Mecca*; and the Grand Signior fets
fuch a Value upon it, that it is Death for a Man to
go within a certain Diftance of the Place where it
is cultivated. The Sultaneffes make great Ufe of it,
and fo do feveral Women in *Conftantinople*, who buy
it very dear from thofe that venture to fteal it.
Might not we produce the fame Effects in *France*
and *England*, by ufing, inftead of the Serquis, a Mixture of a Spirituous Vulnerary Water and common
Water, made after the Manner that I have already
mention'd?

Observation III.

WHEN you want to make a beautiful Paint, observe the following Proportion between the Drugs mention'd in Page 70 of this Work, where this Observation is referr'd to.

Take four Ounces of the Oil of Ben, an Ounce of Virgin Wax, and two Drams and a half of Magistery of Bismuth. The Oil of Ben is preferable to the Oil of sweet Almonds, and also to that of the four Cold Seeds, because it does not over-heat so much as those Oils, and keeps a long time before it changes.

The Magistery of Bismuth is to be preferr'd to that of Tin or Lead, because it is a great deal whiter. This Cosmetic is commonly call'd *Spanish White*. If it be dissolv'd in Flower-de-Luce Water, it will whiten the Face.

An excellent White Paint for the Face.

Take of the white Part of Hartshorn a Pound, of the Flour of Rice two Pounds, of White Lead half a Pound, of Cuttle-Fish Bone two Ounces; Frankincense, Mastich, Gum *Arabic*, of each an Ounce; dilute the Whole in a sufficient Quantity of Rose-Water. Wash the Face therewith.

Red Paint.

The Root of Alkanet gives a handsome red Colour to the Pomatums that are used for the Face. A Scarlet Ribbon dipp'd in common Water, or in Brandy, dy, and rubb'd on the Cheeks, gives them such a beautiful Redness that one would take it to be natural. Others, by rubbing their Cheeks with Scarlet Wool, give them a very handsome Red. Some use Red Lead for the same Purpose.

CINNABAR is composed of Brimstone and Mercury. When it is reduced to a subtil Powder in a Marble Mortar, it acquires so lively and so high a Colour, that it is called Vermilion. Some Ladies mix it with Paint wherewith they rub their Cheeks, which is very dangerous; for by using it frequently they may lose their Teeth, acquire a stinking Breath, and excite a copious Salivation.

The Secret of a Turk *for making an excellent Carmine.*

TAKE a Pound of the best rasp'd *Brasil* Wood, and steep it for three or four Days in a sufficient Quantity of White-Wine Vinegar. After that boil it for half an Hour; strain it through a strong Piece of Linen, and put it again over the Fire. You must likewise dissolve by itself eight Ounces of Alum in a sufficient Quantity of White-Wine Vinegar. Mix both Liquors together, by stirring them in a Mortar; and there will arise a Froth, which is the Carmine. Skim it off, dry it, and keep it for Use. Cochineal or red Sanders may be used instead of *Brasil* Wood.

Another Kind of Red Paint.

TAKE *Brasil* Wood and Roch-Alum, beat them together in a Mortar; boil the Mass in a sufficient Quantity of Red Wine, until one Third is consum'd.

Let

Let the Liquor grow cold, dip therein a Bit of Cotton, and rub it on your Cheeks.

A Kind of Paint that resembles the natural Red.

TAKE Benjamin, *Brasil* Wood, Roch-Alum, of each half an Ounce; of red Sanders an Ounce. Macerate the Whole in a Pint of strong Brandy for the Space of twelve Days; shake the Bottle every Day, let it be well cork'd, and keep it for Use. A slight Touch of this Liquor gives such a beautiful Red to the Cheeks, that it can hardly be distinguish'd from the natural: And what renders this Secret the most valuable is, that its Use is attended with no ill Consequences. Such Women as dare not paint for fear it should be perceived, may use this Composition without any Danger of being suspected.

An Oil for painting the Cheeks red.

TAKE ten Pounds of sweet Almonds, an Ounce of red Sanders in Powder, and an Ounce of Cloves: Beat them well together in a Mortar; pour four Ounces of White Wine thereon, and three Ounces of Rose-Water. Shake the Vessel every Day for eight Days successively; press out the Oil in the same Manner used in making Oil of sweet Almonds.

OBSERVATION IV.

I AM persuaded the Ladies will be well pleased at my translating literally the Manuscript that the Doctor gave the young Odalike. It was transcrib'd

by

by feveral Women in the Seraglio; and I was affur'd
that one which came into my Hands was very exact.
This Manufcript is different from the reft of the
Work, and was written by a different Hand.

The Water of Beauty.

TAKE equal Quantities of Silver-weed and Houfe-
leek; to every Half-Pound add two Drams of Sal
Ammoniac.

The Water of Charms.

TAKE the Sap that weeps from the Vine in the
Months of *May* and *June*, and wafh the Face therewith.

Water to preferve a frefh Complexion.

TAKE three Calves-Feet well chopp'd, three Melons of a middle Size, three Cucumbers, four new-
laid Eggs, a Slice of Pumpkin, two Lemons, a Pint
of Whey, half a Pint of Rofe-Water, a Quart of
Nymphæa Water; Silver-weed and Plantain Water,
of each a Pint; and half an Ounce of Borax. Diftil all thefe Ingredients together in a Sand-Heat.

Water of the Fountain of Youth.

TAKE an Ounce of Sulphur Vivum, two Ounces
of Olibanum and Myrrh, fix Drams of Amber, and
a Pound of Rofe-Water: Diftil the Whole in a Sand-
Heat. Wafh your Face with this Water going to
Bed, the Morning following wafh it with Barley-
Water, and it will look much younger. Some fay
that Pine-Apples produce the fame Effect, and likewife take away Wrinkles. It is alfo faid that the

distill'd

diſtill'd Waters of the Juice of Lemons, of the Whites of Eggs, of Snails, and of Aſſes Milk diſtill'd with Egg-ſhells, are good for the ſame Purpoſe,

An admirable Secret.

AFTER waſhing the Face with Soap and Water, let it be waſh'd over again with the following Lye.

TAKE the Lye that is made of the Aſhes of Vine-Branches, and let it be well clarified; to every Pound add an Ounce of calcined Tartar, two Drams of Sandarach, and the like Quantity of Juniper Gum. Let this Water dry upon your Face without rubbing it, and afterwards waſh it with the following

Imperial Water.

TAKE five Pounds of good Brandy, diſſolve therein Frankincenſe, Maſtich, Benjamin, Gum *Arabic*, of each an Ounce; add half an Ounce of Cloves, an Ounce of Nutmegs, an Ounce and a half of the Kernels of Pine-Apples and of ſweet Almonds, and three Grains of Muſk. Pound them all together in a Mortar, diſtil them afterwards in a Sand-Heat, and keep the Liquor for Uſe.

A very curious Water.

PIMPERNEL Water is ſo excellent for beautifying the Face, that the Lady's Toilet ſhould never be without it.

Excellent Venetian Water.

IN the Month of *May* take two Quarts of Black Cow's Milk; put it into a Bottle with eight Lemons

I and

and four Oranges cut into small Slices; add an Ounce of Sugar-candy, and half an Ounce of Borax. Distil them in a Sand-Heat, or in a Bath-Heat. This Water was counterfeited at *Bagdat* thus:

TAKE twelve Lemons without the Peel, and cut them into Slices, twelve fresh Eggs, six Sheep's-Trotters, four Ounces of Sugar-candy, a large Slice of Melon, the like Quantity of Pumpkin, and two Drams of Borax. Distil them in a Glass Retort with a Leaden Head.

A Refreshing Water.

INFUSE some Wheat Bran for three or four Hours in Vinegar; add some Yolks of Eggs, and a Grain of Ambergrise: Distil all together. This Distillation will yield a most admirable Water for giving a Gloss to the Face. Let it be kept in a Bottle well cork'd, and exposed to the Sun for eight or ten Days.

THE distill'd Water of Melons, of Bean-flowers, of Wild Vine; of green Barley, that is, before the Grain is perfectly form'd, and still milky; and the Water that is found in the Bladders that are form'd in Oaks, produce the same Effect.

A Water that is both sweetening and balsamic.

TAKE the second Barley Water, strain it through a fine Linen Cloth; add thereto some Drops of the Balsam of *Mecca*; shake the Bottle well during the Space of ten or eleven Hours without ceasing, until the Balsam be entirely incorporated with the Water, which happens when the Mixture grows thick. This
Water

Water is something miraculous for its good Property of beautifying the Face, and making it look fresh, fair, and young. If it be used once a Day, it takes away Wrinkles, and gives the Skin a surprizing Lustre. Before using this Water, the Skin is to be wash'd with Rain Water.

A Secret to take away Wrinkles, communicated by a Persian to a Grecian of seventy-two Years of Age, who by the Benefit of it did not seem to be above twenty-five.

PUT a certain Quantity of the Powder of Myrrh upon a Fire-Shovel; when it is red-hot, expose your Face to the Smoke, which you may gather by covering your Head with a Napkin. Repeat this Operation three times; put the Shovel again into the Fire, and when it is quite hot, fill your Mouth with White Wine, and sprinkle the Shovel therewith, and then receive the Smoke as before. Do this three times Morning and Evening as long as you please. The Proprietor of this Secret assures us it will work Miracles.

Another Secret for preserving the Skin of the Face.

WHEN you go to Bed at Night, apply to your Face some Slices of Veal. There is no Topic so efficacious as this for taking away Wrinkles, for keeping the Skin supple, and preserving a fresh Complexion.

A Receipt

A Receipt against the Wrinkles of Women's Breasts, and the Wrinkles on the Belly of those who have had Children.

MELT any Quantity you please of white Wax, and add thereto an equal Quantity of *Sperma Ceti*; incorporate both Ingredients together, and add a small Quantity of Brandy. Dip a Linen Cloth in this Liquor, and apply it to the Belly after Delivery: Bind up the Body with other Cloths. You must turn every Morning the Linen Cloth that was dipp'd in Wax, and renew it every eight Days. This will entirely prevent the Wrinkles, and preserve the Skin smooth and tight. The Cloths that you prepare for the Breasts must have a Hole in the Middle, in order to give a Passage to the Nipples, left they should be too much squeez'd; for too great a Compression of them may produce several fatal Effects.

Virgin's Milk.

THIS Milk is obtain'd by pouring a great deal of Water upon the Dissolution of Lead in Vinegar. The Liquor that results from this Operation is as white as Milk.

Another.

TAKE equal Quantities of Benjamin and Storax; dissolve them in a sufficient Quantity of Spirit of Wine: The Solution will have a reddish Colour, and yield a very sweet Smell. Some add thereto a certain Quantity of the Balsam of *Mecca*. Pour a few Drops of the said Mixture into clear Spring-Water, and stir all together in a proper Vessel: The Mixture

ture will acquire a white Colour. The Ladies use
this Composition with Succefs, to give a good Colour to their Faces.

Another.

REDUCE to Powder three Ounces of the Litharge
of Silver, mix it with an Ounce of good White-Wine
Vinegar, and add an Ounce of common Salt well
pounded and diſſolved in half a Pound of Rain-
Water. Strain the Whole through a Piece of Linen,
and preferve the Liquor in a proper Veſſel, which
you muſt ſhake from time to time. This Liquor will
become as white as Milk. By waſhing therewith
Morning and Evening you will beautify the Skin,
and deſtroy the Freckles, Pimples, and red Spots that
appear on the Forehead and the Cheeks.

Another Kind of Virgin's Milk, that is very eaſily made, and as efficacious as the former.

TAKE what Quantity of Houſe-leek you pleaſe,
beat it in a Marble Mortar, preſs out the Juice, and
clarify it. When you have a mind to uſe it, put a
little of it into a Glaſs, and pour into the Glaſs along
with it ſome Drops of Spirit of Wine. In an Inſtant will be form'd a Kind of curdled Milk, very
proper to make the Skin ſmooth, and to take away
red Spots.

A natural Coſmetic.

THE Water that comes out of a Birch-Tree, by
piercing it in the Spring with an Auger, is deterſive,
and very good for giving the Face a handſome Gloſs.
It is ſaid that the purified Juice of the Leaves of this

I 3   Tree,

Tree, and its diftill'd Water, have the fame Virtue.

Water for whitening the Skin.

TAKE equal Parts of the Roots of Snake-Weed and of the Roots of Daffodil, a Pint of Cow's Milk, and Crumbs of white Bread. Diftil all the Ingredients in a Glafs Alembic, and after the Operation mix the diftill'd Water with an equal Quantity of *Hungary* Water. The diftill'd Water of Fennel and that of white Flower-de-Luce, with a little Maftich, produce the fame Effect. In order to give thefe Waters a fweet Smell, put fome Grains of Mufk into the Neck of the Alembic.

A Water which makes Women more beautiful.

PUT into a Retort five Quarts of Brandy, three Pounds of Crumbs of Bread, fix Ounces of Plum-Tree Gum, four Ounces of the Litharge of Silver, and eight Ounces of fweet Almonds. When the whole is well pounded, digeft it for eight Days, and afterwards diftil it in a Bath-Heat. The Face is to be wafh'd with the Liquor that refults from the Diftillation. Let the Skin imbibe it without rubbing, and it will become charming white.

Another Kind of Water that produces the fame Effect.

TAKE eight Pounds of the Feet and Ears of Hogs and Calves, fix Pounds of Rice Water, two Pounds of Cow's Milk, twelve frefh Eggs, fix Ounces of Crumbs of Bread, a Pound of fine Sugar, and three Pints of Brandy. Mix all together; diftil in a Bath-Heat; and add to the diftill'd Liquor two Ounces of Roch-

Roch-Alum, an Ounce of Borax, two Ounces of Benjamin, and a Dram of Musk. Digest all together in the Sun for the Space of twenty Days; and before you use it, wash your Face with the Decoction of Vermicelli. This Operation is to be repeated Morning and Evening, and it is one of the best Methods that can be used for beautifying the Skin.

Distill'd Water for giving a beautiful Carnation.

Such Ladies as have a disagreeable Colour may use the following Receipt.

Take two Quarts of Vinegar, three Ounces of Mouth-Glue, two Ounces of Nutmegs, six Ounces of common Honey: Distil with a slow Fire; add to the distill'd Liquor a small Quantity of red Sanders, in order to give it a little Colour. Before using it, the Face should be wash'd with Soap-Water, but after using the distill'd Water the Face is not to be wash'd, that it may grow fair and red, and look healthy. This Secret was communicated by a Lady that never fail'd to make use of it, whether she pass'd the Night at Gaming, or whether she was fatigued after a Ball, or after Suppers that are not ended till the first Approach of *Aurora*.

A Composition which gives an admirable Lustre to the Skin.

Take equal Quantities of the Juice of Lemons and of the Whites of Eggs; beat all together in an earthen Pot that is varnish'd, put it over a gentle Fire, and stir it with a wooden Spatula till the whole acquires the Consistence of Butter. Keep it for Use, and

and before you use it you may add to it any Perfume that pleases you best. The Face is to be wash'd with Rice-Water before the Application of it. This is one of the best Compositions that can be used for rendering the Face handsome, bright, and smooth.

Another.

Take a Handful of the Flowers of Beans, of Elder, and Buglofs, and a small Pigeon; cast away the Entrails; add the Juice of two Lemons, four Ounces of Salt, and six Ounces of Camphire: Distil in a Bath-Heat. After the Distillation add some Grains of Musk; expose the Bottle that contains the Liquor to the Sun during the Space of a Month, taking it into the House at Night. Dip therein a small Piece of Linen, and rub the Face therewith very lightly.

Talc *Water.*

All those that make Cosmetics regret very much the Loss of the Secret of making Talc Water. They look'd upon it as one of the most important Discoveries of their whole Art, and the most efficacious for giving a graceful Countenance. Perhaps the following Composition does not differ much from that Water, which was in so much Vogue and Esteem.

Take any Quantity of Talc you please, divide it into Leaves, and calcine it with brown Brimstone. When it is calcinated beat it in a Mortar, pass it through a Sieve, and wash it in a large Quantity of Water. When you are sure you have wash'd away

all

all the Salt, pour off the Water by Inclination. Dry the Sediment that remains in the Bottom; when it is dry, calcine it in a Furnace with a ſtrong Fire, during the Space of two Hours; afterwards take a Pound of this Talc, and reduce it to Powder, with two Ounces of Sal Ammoniac. Put the whole in a Glaſs Bottle, and fix it in a moiſt Place, by which means the Talc will be diſſolved. Pour out the Liquor clear by Inclination, and it will be as tranſparent and as bright as a Pearl. This is the beſt Coſmetic that can be preſented to Ladies of Diſtinction.

Balſamic Water.

TAKE a Pound of *Venice* Turpentine; Oil of Bays, Galbanum, Gum *Arabic*, Gum of Ivy, Frankincenſe, Myrrh, Hepatic Aloes, Aloes Wood, Cloves, the leſſer Comfrey, Cinnamon, Nutmeg, Zedoary, Ginger, white Dittany, of each three Ounces; Borax four Ounces, Muſk a Dram, of Ambergriſe a Scruple. Put the whole into ſix Quarts of Brandy; beat in a Mortar what can be reduced to Powder, and afterwards diſtil. The Balſamic Water that reſults from this Operation fortifies the Parts, and gives them that Vigour and Beauty that are ſo pleaſing to the Eye.

A White Coſmetic Water.

TAKE eight Ounces of bitter Almonds, beat them in a Mortar with two Pounds of Plantain or Roſe Water; afterwards diſſolve therein half a Scruple of corroſive Sublimate, and the Whites of two Eggs.

Water

Water to give a Lustre to the Face.

TAKE two Ounces of Borax, an Ounce of Roch-Alum, two Drams of Camphire; plumous Alum, and burnt Alum, of each an Ounce. Reduce all to Powder, and boil it in a great Quantity of Spring Water. Dilute the White of two Eggs in a small Quantity of Verjuice, put it into the Water when it is taken from the Fire, and expose it to the Sun for the Space of twenty Days. This produces wonderful Effects, and makes the most decay'd Faces look young. Some Ladies wash their Faces with Water wherein Alum has been dissolved. It is true, such Water makes the Skin shine; but it is to be fear'd, that it may at length cause Wrinkles; for Alum is a very powerful Astringent.

A particular Receipt for making the Skin look white.

TAKE equal Quantities of Litharge, Mastich, Olibanum, and Colophony; pound all in a Marble Mortar, and put the Mass into an Alembic, with a sufficient Quantity of White-Wine that has an agreeable Smell. The Water resulting from this Distillation will whiten the Skin in such a manner that several Washings will not be able to rub it off. Others use for the same Purpose Melon Water, Roots of Cuckow-Pint, Lemon Juice, and Goat's Milk, distill'd all together in a Bath-Heat in a Glass Alembic.

An Emollient Pomatum for the Skin.

TAKE any Quantity you please of the Lard of a Boar Pig, cut it into Slices, wash it, and let it ma-

cerate

cerate for nine Days in clean Water, changing the
Water every Day. Afterwards melt it in a Frying-
pan, put the melted Grease into fresh Water, wash
it several times with common Water, and at last with
Rose, Plantain, or Morel Water. Rub your Skin
therewith, and it will become as smooth as Sattin.

Another.

TAKE of the Oil of Poppy-Seed, and of the four
Cold Seeds, of each four Ounces; *Sperma Ceti* six
Drams, white Wax an Ounce. Make of the whole
a Pomatum according to Art.

Oil for cleansing the Face.

PUT into a Quart of sweet Cream any Quantity
you please of the Flowers of white Water-Lily, of
Flower-de-Luce, of Beans, and of Roses. Boil
them all in a Bath-Heat, skim off the Oil that rises
to the Top, preserve it in a Bottle, and expose it to
the Air for some time.

REMARKS.

THE Leaves of Cuckow-Pint laid upon Ulcers
cleanse them in a short time. The distill'd Water
of this Plant is detersive, and cleanses the Face well.
Cæsalpinus says, that the Roots of this Plant are used
in *Italy* to take away the Spots of the Skin; and
there is a white Paint prepared with them much like
white Lead. It is a Kind of Dregs that *Matthiolus*
values much for beautifying the Face. In *Bas-Poitou*
in *France* it is customary with all the Women in the
Country to whiten their Linen with a Paste made of
Cuckow-

Cuckow-Pint. They cut the Stalk of this Plant (when it flowers) into small Bits, and macerate it three Weeks in Water, which they change every Day; then they reduce the Sediment into a Paste, and dry it for Use.

An excellent Paint for the Face.

TAKE any Quantity you please of Sheep's Trotters well chopp'd; break the long Bones in order to get out the Marrow. But that you may effect it with greater Facility, macerate the Bones for a Day or two in Water, which you must change three or four times a Day. Keep the Vessel in a Cellar; and to every Dozen of Sheep's-Trotters add half a Dozen Calves-Feet. When you have obtain'd their Marrow, wash it several times, renewing the Water each time. Repeat the Washing till it becomes very white; and also wash the Bones well, after taking out the Marrow, and boil them in clear Water for an Hour or two. Strain through a Linen Cloth; and let the liquid Part, that passes through, settle for twelve Hours. Take off with a Silver Spoon the Oil that comes to the Top, and mix it with the Marrow which you have prepared as above. Melt the whole over a gentle Fire, and for every four Ounces add an Ounce of Borax, and the like Quantity of Roch-Alum burnt. When the whole is sufficiently hot, add two Ounces of the Oil of the four Cold Seeds press'd without the Help of Fire, and a small Quantity of Kid's-Grease. Strain through a Piece of clean Linen, and keep it for Use. Some, instead of Kid's-Grease, use a small Quantity of Wax

or

or Sheep's Tallow; but the Wax dries and chaps the Skin, and the Sheep's Tallow grows reddish, and makes the Face look yellow.

The Handkerchief of Venus.

CALCINATE any Quantity you please of the Chalk of *Briançon*; afterwards macerate it in strong Brandy, wherein you are to dip your Cloth, and then let it dry under a Shade: Repeat the Operation three times. The Handkerchiefs which are made of this Cloth hardly receive any Dirt.

Another more compound Method of preparing it.

TAKE of Roch-Alum two Pounds, of Borax a Pound; Gum *Arabic* and Gum Tragacanth, of each four Pounds: Infuse the whole in two Pounds of Malmsey and two Quarts of Goat's Milk. Take two Pounds of Ceruse, tie it up in a Piece of Linen, boil it in a sufficient Quantity of common Water, and pour the said Water upon the foregoing Infusion. After that take two Pounds of white Honey, and three Pounds of Turpentine, and as much of fine Sugar; boil them in a sufficient Quantity of White-Wine Vinegar distill'd, and when it is consumed to half, add it to the foregoing Mixture. Add also three Ounces of Myrrh reduced to fine Powder, and several Snails without the Shells, and well wash'd in common Water. Shake the Vessel for half an Hour, that the Ingredients may be well mix'd. Put the whole into a Retort with a fat Pullet well clean'd and cut into small Pieces, an Ounce of Camphire, the White of ten fresh Eggs, the Peel of five Oranges,

and diftil. The firft Water that comes off in the Diftillation will be very clear; keep it apart. The fecond Water will be very white, and is that which is
to be ufed in making the Handkerchief after the following Manner. Take fine Cloth, wafh it in Rofe-
Water, and let it dry; afterwards fteep it for four
and twenty Hours in the foregoing white Water, and
let it dry under a Shade. When you have a mind
to try the wonderful Effects of the Handkerchief, let
your Face be clean before you rub it therewith, and
it will render the Skin as bright and as fmooth as
Sattin. This Handkerchief may be carried in the
Pocket. Its good Effects in general are well known,
but more particularly when the Face is rubb'd with
it after fweating.

Varnifh for the Face.

PUT into a Bottle twelve Ounces of Brandy, an
Ounce of Sandarach, and half an Ounce of Benjamin. Shake the Bottle often, and afterwards let it
fettle. When you ufe it, wafh your Face beforehand, and it will give it the handfomeft Luftre ima-
ginable.

Salt of Liverwort, *which is of excellent Service for preferving the beautiful Colour of the Face, or for recovering it when it is impaired or loft.*

TAKE of the Roots of Agrimony two Pounds; of
the Roots of Succory and Viper-Grafs, of each a
Pound; of bitter Coftus, Eryngo, and Turmeric, of
each half a Pound; Sweet-Cane, Rhapontic, of each
four Ounces; *Roman* Wormwood, Southernwood,
Maudlin,

Maudlin, Spleenwort, Veronica, Water-Liverwort, Fumitory, Dodder, of each three Ounces. Calcine the whole in a Reverberatory Furnace, afterwards add the Afhes of Rhubarb and of Caffia-Bark, of each an Ounce and a half; digeft the whole in a Decoction of the Flowers of Liverwort, and draw off the Salt according to Art. This Salt helps the Circulation of the Bile, removes Obftructions, cures the Jaundice, takes away the livid Colour of the Face, and gives the Skin an agreeable Vermilion-Colour. The Dofe of this Salt is from twenty-four to thirty-fix Grains in a convenient Vehicle.

A remarkable Secret.

MAKE a Hole in a Lemon, fill it with Sugar-candy, cover it with Leaf-Gold, and over the faid Gold apply the Part of the Peel you have cut off; afterwards roaft your Lemon under warm Afhes. When you have a mind to make ufe of it, fqueeze out a little of the Juice through the Hole you have already made, receive the Juice on a clean Cloth, and rub your Face therewith. This Juice is very efficacious for cleanfing the Skin, and rendering the Complexion bright and fair.

Oil of Tartar, for rendering the Face both white and fair.

TAKE three Pounds of the Tartar of White-Wine, four Ounces of Nitre, three Ounces of Pewter calcined, and an Ounce of Roch-Alum. Beat all together in a Mortar, put them into an earthen Difh, and expofe it to a Reverberatory Heat till the Mafs

be

be thoroughly calcined: Infufe an Ounce of the cal-cined Mafs in a Pint of Brandy. This Infufion is one of the beft Cofmetics that are employ'd for whitening the Face, and for preferving that natural Frefhnefs which excites the Defires of the moft in-fenfible Hearts.

Oil of Pearls.

Put upon a Plate any Quantity you pleafe of Pearls, and pour over them fome good diftill'd Vi-negar. When the Pearls are diffolved, add a fmall Quantity of Gum *Arabic*. Keep the Solution for Ufe. Wafh your Face before you bathe it with this Solution; which will foon dry of itfelf. This is one of the beft Secrets that have been invented for ren-dering the Face both white and fair.

A Pafte for the Hands.

Take of fweet Almonds a Pound; White-Wine Vinegar, Spring-Water, and Brandy, of each a Quartern; of Crumbs of Bread a Quarter of a Pound, and the Yolk of two Eggs.

The fweet Almonds are to be blanched, and af-terwards beat in a Mortar, and fprinkled with Vine-gar, that the Pafte may not turn into Oil. Add the Crumbs of Bread after being moiften'd with Brandy; mix them with the fweet Almonds and the Yolk of Eggs. Boil all over a gentle Fire, ftirring them con-tinually, left the Pafte fhould ftick to the Bottom of the Pan. Others make it after the following Man-ner. Take fweet and bitter Almonds, of each two Ounces; the Kernels of Pine-Apples, and the four

Cold

Cold Seeds, of each an Ounce; beat all together in
a Mortar, and afterwards add the Yolks of two Eggs,
and the Crumb of white Bread. Pour in a sufficient Quantity of White-Wine Vinegar to moisten
the Ingredients, and put all into a Pan, which warm
over a gentle Fire. Remove the Pan from the Fire
when the Paste begins to boil.

Another.

TAKE of sweet Almonds a Pound, of the Kernels of Pine-Apples four Ounces; beat all in a Mortar, add two Ounces of fine Sugar, an Ounce of
white Honey, an Ounce of the Meal of Beans, and
two Ounces of Brandy.

Another.

TAKE a Pound of Almonds, an Ounce of yellow
Sanders and Iris, two Ounces of Sweet-Cane; pour
in two Glasses of Rose-Water, add a Pippin cut into
small Pieces, a Quarter of a Pound of Crumbs of
white Bread well dried; make all into a Paste with
two Ounces of Gum Tragacanth dissolved in Rose-
Water, and keep it for Use.

Another.

TAKE any Quantity you please of Quinces, pare
them, pound them in a Mortar, and sprinkle them
with Rose-Water and White-Wine; add the Crumb
of white Bread, Almonds beat in a Mortar together
with White-Wine, and a small Quantity of white
Soap. Boil over a slow Fire, and keep the Paste
for Use.

Another.

Another.

INFUSE sweet Almonds, after they are beat in a Mortar, for two or three Hours in Goat's Milk or Cow's Milk; pass them through a Linen Cloth with strong Expression; put the strain'd Liquor over the Fire, and add half a Pound of white Bread, two Drams of Borax, and the like Quantity of Roch-Alum calcined. Towards the End add an Ounce of *Sperma Ceti*; stir the Ingredients well with a Spatula, and let them boil well together.

White Soap.

THIS Soap is made with one Part of the Lye of the Ashes of *Spanish* Glass-Wort and Quick-Lime, and two Parts of the Oil of Olives, or of the Oil of sweet Almonds.

Wash-balls of Bologne.

TAKE a Pound of *Genoa* Soap cut into small Pieces, and four Ounces of Lime; pour thereon a Quartern of Brandy, let it ferment for four and twenty Hours, then spread out the Mass upon a Leaf of Paper, and let it dry. When it is dry, pound it in a Marble Mortar, with an Ounce of the Wood of St. *Lucia*, an Ounce and a half of yellow Sanders, half an Ounce of Iris, and as much of Sweet-Cane. All these Ingredients should be reduced to Powder beforehand. Make the whole into a Paste with the White of some Eggs, and four Ounces of Gum Tragacanth diluted in Rose-Water. Form the Mass into Wash-balls.

Wash-balls

Wash-balls of the Seraglio.

TAKE a Pound of Iris, four Ounces of Benjamin, two Ounces of Storax, and as much of yellow Sanders, half an Ounce of Cloves, a Dram of Cinnamon, a small Quantity of Lemon-Peel, an Ounce of Mahalel or Wood of St. *Lucia*, and one Nutmeg. Reduce all to Powder; then take about two Pounds of white Soap grated, which you are to infuse for four or five Days in three Pints of Brandy with the foregoing Powder. Reduce the whole into a Paste with about a Quart of Orange-Flower Water. Mix with the said Paste a sufficient Quantity of Starch, and reduce the Mass into Wash-balls of any Bulk you think proper, adding thereto the Whites of Eggs and Gum Tragacanth dissolv'd in Sweet-scented Water. If you have a mind to render your Wash-balls still more odoriferous, you must incorporate in the Paste some Grains of Musk, or the Essential Oil of Lavender, of Bergamot, of Daisies, of Jasmine, of Cloves, of Cinnamon, or, in a Word, that whose Smell pleases you best.

Sweet Bags, to give a good Smell to Linen.

TAKE Roses dried under a Shade, Clove Gilliflowers bruised, and Flowers of Nutmeg; mix all together, and put them into a Bag.

A dry Popouri, *composed for Despoine* MARY *by her First Physician.*

TAKE of Orange-Flowers a Pound; of common Roses, from which separate the Heels, a Pound; of red

red Daisies, deprived also of the white Pedicles that are at the Bottom of the Leaves, half a Pound; Sweet Marjoram, Myrrh pick'd, of each a Pound; red Roses, Thyme, Lavender, Rosemary, Sage, Chamomile, Melilot, Hyssop, Sweet Balm, Balm-Mint, of each two Ounces; of Laurel, fifteen or twenty Leaves; of Jasmine two or three Handfuls; Lemon-Peel a good Handful, and as much of green Oranges; of Salt half a Pound. Put all into a Vessel, let them remain so during a Month, stirring them twice every Day with a wooden Spoon. At the End of the Month add of Iris in Powder twelve Ounces, and the like Quantity of Benjamin; Cloves and Cinnamon in Powder, of each two Ounces; Mace, Storax, Sweet-Cane, the Powder of *Cyprus*, of each one Ounce; yellow Sanders and Cyperus, of each six Drachms. Mix all together as before, and you will have a *Popouri* that will yield a very agreeable Smell, and that never receives any Damage by Time.

A Bag of an agreeable Smell.

TAKE of Florentine Orris a Pound and a half, of Rose-Wood six Ounces, of Sweet-Cane half a Pound, of yellow Sanders four Ounces, of Benjamin five Ounces, Cloves half an Ounce, and Cinnamon an Ounce. Reduce all to a Powder, and fill your Bags therewith.

A Perfuming-Pan.

BOIL two Ounces of Storax in half a Pint of Rose-Water, together with four Ounces of Benjamin.

min. Put into a Nodule of new Linen twelve Cloves,
a Dram of Ladanum, as much of Sweet-Cane, and
a little Orange-Peel. Cover the Pot well, let it boil
for a long time, ſtrain it through a Cloth without
ſtrong Expreſſion, take out the Sediment, and preſerve it in a ſmall Box.

Sweet Balls of an agreeable Smell.

TAKE two Ounces of Benjamin, half an Ounce
of Storax, a Dram of Aloes-Wood, twenty Grains
of good Civet, a little Willow-Bark, and ſome fine
Sugar. Boil the whole in a ſufficient Quantity of
Roſe-Water.

IF you have a mind to give your Balls a ſweeter
Smell, add twelve Grains of Ambergriſe when the
Cake is almoſt baked. Reduce all into a Maſs, and
form your Paſtils.

Paſtils that are very odoriferous, and much uſed in Fumigation.

TAKE of the pureſt Ladanum, and of Benjamin,
of each four Ounces; Cane-Storax, and dry Balſam
of *Peru*, of each an Ounce and a half; of the Gum
of Tacamahaca four Ounces, of Olibanum a Dram
and a half, of the beſt Myrrh a Dram, of the liquid Balſam of *Peru* an Ounce, Ambergriſe four
Drams, Muſk and Civet of each two Scruples; of
the eſſential Oil of the Wood of Rhodium a Dram;
of that of the Flowers of Oranges, of Lemons, of
Bergamot, of each ſixteen Drops; of that of Cinnamon, and of Cloves, of each eight Drops; of
the Powder of Gum Lac five Ounces; Caſcarilla,

Aloes-

Aloes-Wood, Rhodium-Wood, the Wood of St. *Lucia*, yellow Sanders, Cinnamon, Cloves, of each two Drams. Reduce all into a Mass in a Bath-Heat, and form it into Pastils according to Art.

A Method of making different Kinds of Sweet Bags.

FOR making Sweet Bags you may use all the different Parts of aromatic Plants: As the *Leaves* of Southernwood, Tarragon, the Balsam-Tree, Wild Mint and Crisped Mint, Dittany, Ivy, Ground-Ivy, Laurel, Hyssop, Lovage, Sweet Marjoram, Wild Marjoram, Balm, Poley-Mountain, Thyme, Rosemary, Sage, Savory, Scordium, Cedar, the Lemon-Tree, Saffron, Lavender, Roses, Lily of the Valley, red Pinks, yellow Gilli-flowers, Jonquils, the Lime-Tree, and of Mace. *Fruits*; such as the Seeds of Fennel, Aniseed, &c. the Peel of Lemons and green Oranges; the Berries of Juniper, Nutmegs, Cloves. *Roots*; such as those of Sweet-Cane, the *Bohemian* Angelica, the Eastern Costus, the Cyperus, the Iris, Zedoary. *Woods*; as those of Rhodium, Juniper, Cinnamon, and St. *Lucia. Gums*; as Frankincense, Myrrh, Styrax, Benjamin, Ambergrise, and Amber.

ALL these Drugs should be well dried, and preserved in a dry Place. Put a little Quantity of common Salt along with them, for fear they should grow mouldy; and if you have a Liking for any particular Smell, you must add a great Quantity of that Ingredient whose Odour pleases you most.

THE

THE
LIBRARY
OF THE
TOILET.

WATERS.

WATER of Silver-
weed,
of Cedar,
without Equal,
of the Queen of
Hungary,
wherein the Lemon
predominates,
wherein the Berga-
mot abounds,
wherein the Cedar
is superior,
wherein the Amber
prevails,
of Balm,
of *Luze*,
Vulnerary,

Water of Roſes,
Plantain,
Jonquil,
Violet,
Pink,
Jaſmine,
Orange-flower,
Bergamot,
Yarrow,
Scurvy-graſs,
Myrtle,
Angelica,
Honey,
Engliſh,
without Odour,
Lavender,
Simple,

Water

Water of Lavender diftill'd,
Red,
Barbel,
Bean,
Lettuce,
Eyebright,
of the Sultanesses,
of *Cordoua*,
of *Portugal*,
for a Marshal's Lady,

Water of *Popouri*,
of the smaller Lemons,
of Brandy,
Simple,
with Camphire,
Perfumed,
of Guaiacum,
of Strawberries,
of *Cyprus*,
of Ambret,
of Florentine Orris.

S P I R I T S.

Spirit of Wine,
Rectified,
without Smell,
with Cedar,
with Bergamot,
with Lavender,
with Musk,
with Amber,
with Camphire,
of Alum,

Spirit of Wormwood,
of Amber,
Volatile, Oily, Aromatic,
of Rosemary,
of Juniper,
of Orange-Peel,
of Lemon-Peel,
of Scurvy-grafs,
of Cherries.

E S S E N C E S.

Essence of Lemons,
of Bergamot,
of Cedar,
of Oranges,
of the smaller Lemons,
of Jasmine,
of *Spanish* Jasmine,
of *Nerolé*,

Essence of Pinks,
of Gilli-flowers,
of Cinnamon,
of Ben,
of Amber,
of Roses,
of Lavender,
of Anifeed,
of Fennel.

ALUMS.

ALUMS.

Alum Simple,
  Calcin'd,
  with Pink,

Alum with Violet,
  with Amber,
  for a Marſhal's Lady;

SPUNGES.

Fine Spunges prepar'd,
  for the Body,

Spunges for the Teeth,
  for the Beard.

POMATUMS.

Pomatum Simple,
  White,
  Red,
  Yellow,
  of Cucumbers,
  of Snails,
  of the four Cold
    Seeds,
  for the Chaps of the
    Lips,
  with the Flowers of
    Oranges,
  with Bergamot,
  with Lemons,
  of green Walnuts,
  with Jaſmine,
  with the leſſer Le-
    mons,
  with Lavender,

Pomatum with Pink,
  with Violet,
  with Tuberoſe,
  with Jonquil,
  with Sheep's Trot-
    ters,
  with Cedar,
  with the Caſſias,
  of *Frangipane*,
  with Amber,
  of *Portugal*,
  of *Italy*,
  of *Rome*,
  of *Provence*,
  of the White of
    Pearls,
  in a Cane,
  in a Pot.

OILS.

Oil of ſweet Almonds,
  of bitter Almonds,
  preſs'd without Fire,

Oil of Hazel,
  of Ben,
  of Poppies,

L

Oil

Oil of Flower-de-Luce,   Oil of Storax,
    of Roses,   of Tartar *per Deli-*
    of Cinnamon,   *quium.*

V I N E G A R S.

VINEGAR of Roses,   Vinegar of *Surat,*
    of the Four Rob-   *Roman,*
    bers,   of *Venus.*

P A S T E S.

PASTE of sweet Almonds,   Paste Liquid,
    of bitter Almonds,   Greasy,
    of dried Almonds,   Yellow with Honey,
    of sweet and bitter   for the Queen,
    Almonds,   with Soap.

W A S H - B A L L S.

WASH-BALLS Common,   Wash-balls Light,
    of pure Soap,   Heavy,
    of odoriferous Soap,   Amber'd,
    Marbled of *Pro-*   with Lavender,
     vence,   Grey with Laven-
    of pure *Neapolitan*   der,
     Soap,   with Amber,
    Perfumed,   with Lemon,
    of *Bologne,*   with Bergamot,
    of *Frangipane,*   of *Neroli,*
    White,   of Amber.
    Brown,

P O W D E R S.

POWDER Common,   Powder purified with Spi-
    very Fine,   rit of Wine,
    purified with Bran-   White,
    dy,   Black,

                                    Powder

Powder Brown,
Fair,
Grey,
Flesh-colour'd,
Rose-colour'd,
Cherry-colour'd,
for a Marshal's Lady,
with Violet,
with Orris,

Powder with Pink,
Orange-flower,
of Jonquil,
of Tuberose,
of Yarrow,
of Beans,
English,
Cyprus,
Bright of all Colours.

RED PAINT.

RED in a Pot,
in Powder,
for the Fair,
for the Brown,
with different Colours,
of *Paris*,

Red of *Spain*,
of *Portugal*,
of *Nismes*,
Carmine,
Fire,
Rose,
of different Colours.

GLOVES *and* MITTENS.

GLOVES and MITTENS
of *Provence*,
of *Grenoble*,
of *Avignon*,
of *Blois*,
of *Vendôme*,
English,
of Buff,
of Shamoy,

Ditto of Castor-skin,
of Deer-skin,
of Dog's-skin,
Leather,
Fat,
Dry,
Trimm'd, or
Not trimm'd.

HEAD-BANDS for the Wrinkles of the Forehead.
Depilatory Wax.

P A T C H E S.

PATCHES of Velvet,   Patches Superfine,
    of Sattin,   Unmatch'd.
    of Taffety,

T O O T H - P I C K E R S.

Common,
Fine,
Carmeline,

For the T E E T H.

Spunges,   Dragon's-Blood,
Liquors,   Simple,
Roots of Marſh-mallows,   Perfumed,
    Simple,   Powders,
    Prepared,   Opiates.
    Red,
    Coral,

B A G S.

BAGS of *England*,   Herbs aromatic of *Mont-*
    of *Montpelier*,   *pelier*,
    Sultaneſs's, and Baſ- Dry Lavender,
        kets of Odour,   Porte-feuille prick'd, gar-
Pockets odoriferous,   niſh'd with Plants.

V I R G I N's M I L K.

White,
Red,
Of *Rome*.

P A I N T.

White of Pearls,
White of different Kinds.

P A S T I L S.

PASTILS.

PASTILS Odoriferous,   Paſtils with Violet,
    to burn,   with Bergamot,
    of *Portugal*,   with Lemons.
    of Cachoo,

STAYS, or BODICE, ſtuck with the fine Herbs of
                Montpelier,
    Pockets,
    Stomachers,
    Porte-feuille, ſtuck at the ſame Place.

A B D E K E R :

O R,

The ART of preserving

B E A U T Y.

PART II.

CHAPTER I.

Of CHRYSOLITE'S *Intrigue.*

AB D E K E R withdrew to the Porch, and sat down upon a Sopha. Enchanted by the Charms of *Fatima*, he studied to contrive Means to reveal his Love. *Chrysolite* followed him immediately to the same Place, and seated herself by his Side. It is in vain, said she, for you to endeavour to hide your Passion in the inward Recesses of your Heart; for many Sparks of Love, which issue from your Eyes, have kindled a Flame in the Breast of *Fatima.* I have plainly perceived the Truth of

what

what I advance. Your Difcourfe, your conftant At-
tendance, your Countenance, your Carriage, and all
your Actions, are fo many Proofs thereof, that I am
fully convinced of what I fay. The young Odalike, who adores you, could not conceal her predo-
minant Paffion. She let me into a Part of the Secret, and I foon comprehended the reft. Fear not;
I am difcreet; you may declare your Mind to me
with full Confidence. My dear *Chryfolite*, how fhall
I tell you, replied *Abdeker?* I have no Terms ftrong
enough to exprefs the Violence of my Love. *Fatima*
is the Soul that gives me Life; fhe is, in regard to
me, that Heaven which the great Prophet *Mahomet*
promifes to his faithful Servants. You have imprudently difcover'd your Secret, anfwer'd *Chryfolite*:
Liften, however, to what I have to fay. What, do
you intend to betray me, replied *Abdeker?* Be gone;
think that my Life is not fo dear to me as my Love.
You may declare all to the Emperor; but I fhall die
with Pleafure, fince I have heard that I am belov'd
by *Fatima*, and fhe knows that I love her. She will
at leaft be informed, that he who expired in the
midft of Torments died a Sacrifice to her Love.
But what do I fay? fenfelefs as I am! I hope you
will not betray a Love fo pure and difinterefted as
mine. My Life will not be fufficient to appeafe the
Fury of *Mahomet*: His Cruelty will extend farther;
he will alfo facrifice the Life of innocent *Fatima* as
a Victim to his Tyranny. How fhall I diffuade you
from fo dreadful a Difcovery? Liften, replied *Chryfolite*, and you fhall know what you are to do. You
have given a full Explanation of the Caufe of the
Diforder

Disorder that has given so fatal a Stroke to my Charms. *Fatima* seem'd to be so well persuaded of it, that she mention'd me as an Example. Yes, *Abdeker*, it is Love which has made all that Havock, as you have truly discover'd by your Art: But you could not find out, by Sensation or Sympathy, that you are the Person whom I adore. You have a long while attracted my Eyes, and yet I never could obtain from you a favourable Glance. Your Eyes are continually directed towards the young Odalike, and it is in vain for *Chrysolite* to attempt to conquer your Heart. I smother my Sighs Night and Day; you are the only Object of my Thoughts; my Eye-lids are no longer closed in Slumbers; the most delicate Food has something in it that seems nauseous; and besides I eat, like a senseless Wretch, Things that Nature never design'd for the Stomach: In fine, I languish, I die for Love. The Signs of it are so evident, that you cannot doubt of it; and even if you were not told it beforehand, you might read in my Countenance that your own Person is the only Object of my Love.

PERCEIVING that *Abdeker* was speechless, and returned no Answer to her Discourse, she went on in the following Manner. As you are now apprized of the true Nature of my Disorder, it is your Duty to dry up its Source: It is your Duty, I say, since it is you who have undertaken a Cure; and, as a Recompense for your Compliance, I will favour your Proceedings in regard to *Fatima*. But as I am likely to see my Love despised afterwards, I will at least have the Satisfaction to see it crown'd before that of

my

my Rival. You remain dumb! You are at a Stand!
I have only one Word to add farther: Call to mind
the engaging *Zinzima*, for whom you have formerly
fhew'd a Concern.

SHE herfelf was the very Perfon; for *Azor* died
foon after he married her, and *Zinzima* was obliged
to defcend to the Condition of a Slave. Her Father,
who was Boftangi, and very much in favour with
the Grand Signior, engaged his Highnefs to buy her,
to ferve the Women of the Seraglio. She was the
Perfon that *Mahomet* appointed chiefly to attend on
Fatima. The Doctor muft be highly furprifed when
he met *Zinzima* in this Place, efpecially when he
confider'd that he had to deal with a Woman that
was capable of forming the moft fubtil and the moft
refolute Projects, and that would undertake any thing
in order to accomplifh her Defign. The long Inter-
val of Time fince he faw her, the Change of her
Condition, her different Drefs, the Alteration of her
Countenance, the Want of Attention, his extraordinary Occupations, his Love, and feveral other Circumftances, hinder'd him from knowing her before;
but the prefent Conjuncture made him foon call her
to mind. Uncertain what Refolution to take, and
greatly fearing the Intrigues of *Chryfolite*, he thought
the moft prudent Method would be to flatter her
Hopes. If formerly, faid he, I have fupported the
Intereft of *Zinzima*, I fhall do no lefs this Day for
Chryfolite: She was heretofore able to refift *Azor*;
why fhould fhe hinder me now from preferving all
my Flame for *Fatima*? Love is not difpofed of at
pleafure; one cannot direct it to a determin'd Ob-

ject

ject fo often as Prudence might fuggeft. I know very well that there is fome internal Principle, which
engages every one willingly to love thofe who love
him : Love is the moft lawful Tribute that can be
paid to Love. You may therefore depend upon my
Acknowledgment; and perhaps Time may produce
more lively Sentiments, that will oblige me one Day
to recompenfe the Conftancy of *Chryfolite.*

THIS Day feem'd to *Chryfolite* to be too remote;
but feeing the firft and moft difficult Step was taken,
fhe refolved not to fuffer the Impreffion of the Stroke
fhe had given to diminifh. The devouring Flame
that confumed her would not permit her to liften to
Reafon, nor to be foothed by Promifes. Come, fays
fhe, follow me. *Abdeker* forefaw all that was to be
feared from an offended Lover; he follow'd her
without afking any farther Queftion; they enter'd
the Garden of the Seraglio, and after croffing an
Avenue of Cyprefs, they pafs'd under a Bower of
Myrtle. *Chryfolite* ftopp'd and embraced the Doctor,
who was in a deep Confternation. She careffed him
fo much, that he was foon convinced how difficult it
is to refift an Object deeply in Love. This is the
firft Step, dear *Fatima,* cried he, that I am to take
in order to obtain you: *Chryfolite* is a Step of the
Throne I am to afcend. What does it avail me,
fays *Chryfolite* with Emotion, to hear you pronounce
the Name of the young Odalike, at the delightful
Moment wherein I hoped that all your Senfes would
be employ'd in anfwering my Expectations? However, I will overlook this Imprudence, provided the
Satisfaction of my Love is not neglected. Your
                                        Compliance

Compliance will give a new Luftre to your Science:
For *Fatima*, whofe Name is fo dear to you, will
publifh both far and near that you have reftored
Chryfolite to all her Charms; and *Chryfolite* will applaud privately the efficacious Remedy that her Phyfician has employ'd for difperfing the Clouds which
veiled her Face.

A B D E K E R thought it the fafeft Way to endeavour to pleafe her. She feem'd to be one of the
Prieftelfes of *Bacchus*, that defcend from Mount *Cy-
theron*. When the Affair was over, and fhe had recover'd from her Tranfports, fhe conducted the Doctor through By-paths out of the Seraglio.

C H A P. II.

Of the Diforders of the S K I N.

IT was in vain that *Fatima* waited for *Abdeker* in
the Porch. She was obliged to come back to
her Apartment accompanied only by fome of her
Maids. Soon after *Chryfolite* came to her, and fpoke
fo much in Praife of the Doctor, that fhe feem'd to
be in an enthufiaftic Tranfport. The young Odalike was charm'd to hear her talk in that Manner,
and was overjoy'd to fee that fhe made fo great an
Account of her Lover. It was adding new Fuel to
her Flame, and was the fureft Way of giving her
Pleafure.

A B D E K E R was much furprifed at fuch an odd
Adventure, and endeavour'd to conceal it from his
Miftrefs,

Miſtreſs. He paſs'd two Days without going to the
Seraglio, which ſo much alarm'd the young Odalike, that ſhe enquired of *Chryſolite* a hundred times
a Day if ſhe knew the Cauſe of his Abſence. Oh,
how long do the Days ſeem, ſaid ſhe, to ſeparated
Lovers; but how ſhort do they appear when they
are both together! As ſhe ſpoke thus, *Abdeker* appear'd. She cried out, My dear *Abdeker*, I am
revived: I perceive the Light that enlivens my
Senſes. *Abdeker*, you might eaſily know, as well
by my Countenance as by my Diſcourſe, that your
Perſon was not indifferent. If I had any Room in
your tender Affection, how is it poſſible you could
paſs ſo long a Time without ſeeing me? Could you
abſent yourſelf, without the utmoſt Grief and Sor-
row, from the Object of your Love? The bright
Luminary of the Day has paſs'd twice through our
Zenith ſince I ſaw you, except in my Dreams and
in my Imagination. Can I judge of the Heart of
others by my own? I think Love ſhould render you
more lively and more impatient. The Doctor was
at a loſs for a reaſonable Excuſe againſt ſo juſt a
Reproach. My dear *Fatima*, ſaid he, the Tenderneſs
I have for you is not fictitious: You can eaſily judge
of it, becauſe you could diſcover it before I had the
Courage to declare it. I call *Chryſolite* to witneſs;
ſhe knows how many hard Conflicts my Heart has
been engaged in on your Account. *Chryſolite* did
not think it convenient to liſten to the reſt of their
Diſcourſe. She retired immediately, in order to
give more Liberty to her Miſtreſs to ſpeak her Mind.
My Love for you, continued the Doctor, is ſo pure

M   and

and full of Refpect, that I am afraid of incurring
your Difpleafure, if I fhould have the Rafhnefs to
make you any Propofals that were not to your
Liking; for to be in Difgrace with you would be
my Ruin and utter Overthrow.——But why have
you pafs'd two Days without coming to fee me, replied *Fatima?* You know the Weaknefs of my Con-
ftitution, and yet you abandon me at a Time when
I have moft Need of your Advice. Indeed I think
it fhews how much you neglect the Care you ought
to have of my Health, and what little Account you
make of my Charms, when you expofe them to a
thoufand Infirmities, which your very Prefence would
diffipate. Sure this is very ill-becoming a Phyfician that pretends to know the Value of Beauty.

THESE Reproaches, replied *Abdeker,* would feem
lefs fenfible to me, if I was lefs intent upon your
Beauty. In the midft of all the Cares and Occupations that my Profeffion requires, you are always
prefent to my Mind; and I willingly embrace all
Occafions of pleafing you. Yefterday, among the
great Number of Patients that I was obliged to vifit
in *Pera* *, I made fome Obfervations upon fuch
Difeafes of the Skin as caufe Deformities in the
Face. You feem'd to be very attentive to the different Subjects of our former Converfations. You
are willing to know all the Caufes that can any way
prove prejudicial to Beauty. Therefore I think it is
giving you new Proofs of my Zeal, if I endeavour

---

* The Suburbs of *Conftantinople,* where the Minifters of fo-
reign Princes are lodged.

to satisfy you in that Article; though I cannot do
it without depriving myself of the greatest Pleasure
in Life, which is to observe your Charms with full
Attention, to hear you speak, and to read in your
Eyes that you are not indifferent about your Physician. I applaud your Reasons, replied *Fatima*; yet
still I had Cause to be impatient about your Absence. However, to atone for all the Trouble and
Disquiet you have given me, I require you to communicate the Observations of which you have
spoken; for I am always curious about what regards
your Science, and about the Means of preserving
Beauty.

THE first Patient that I saw, says *Abdeker*, was a
Woman whose Face was all red, and full of red
Pustules. The Physicians call this Distemper the
Gutta Rosacea. Sometimes it appears like Drops of
Blood spread over the Skin, and it often gives an
unequal Redness to the Nose and Cheeks. Some-
times the Nose and Face become so big and so mon-
strous, that it is frightful to behold them. This
Disease seldom attacks Persons that live soberly; it
is common among such as make immoderate Use of
Spirituous Liquors; and it is epidemic among the
Inhabitants of *Frifeland* and those of the *Low Countries*, on account of drinking too much Wine and
Drams. There have been some Drunkards that
have had this Disorder to such a Degree, that the
Blood has issued in abundance from their Noses as
they sat at Table, and hinder'd them some Minutes
from drinking; but after the Hæmorrhage ceases,
some retake their Glass, drink about with new Vi-

gour,

gour, and never give over till their Face is like a
Firebrand. Yesterday I prescribed for the Woman
at *Pera* a moist emollient Diet; I order'd her to ab-
stain from Coffee, and advised her to apply a Lini-
ment to her Face made of the White of an Egg,
together with small Quantities of Alum and of Camphire, and afterwards to make use of the Oil of
Myrrh, which is very efficacious in such Cases. *

After that I visited another Woman, whose
Body was all cover'd over with Pimples. These
Pimples are small Eminences that appear upon the
Surface of the Skin, and render it rough and un-
even. They are almost always produced by a bilious and acrimonious Sweat. If they do not go off
of their own accord, the Patient must have recourse
to a diluting and mucilaginous Diet, in order to
blunt the Points of the sharp and acrimonious Particles that obstruct and irritate the Capillaries, and
with the Intention of diluting the Bile that cannot
pass through its usual Passages, on account of an
extraordinary Cohesion or Consistence it acquires by
some unusual Accident. It is good to make frequent
Use of cold icy Drink, to keep the Body at Rest,
to remain in a cold Place, to drink Water in which
Nitre is dissolved, Whey, some Glasses of Barley-
Water, Limonade, and Chicken-Broth with the four
Cold Seeds, in order to temper the Acrimony of the
Blood. The Patient may also wash with a Decoction of Linseed and that of Marsh-mallows; and
with Rose-Water, wherein must be dissolved a small

* See Observation I.

Quantity

Quantity of the Sugar of Lead. You may also employ with Succefs Waters, Pomatums, and sweetening Soaps, which are to be applied to the Part of the Skin that is attack'd by this Diforder.

In the fame Perfon's Houfe I was confulted by a Woman who had Sapphires on her Face. As they were very troublefome, fhe was defirous to get rid of them. Sapphires are red and hard Eminences, white at their Point; they are commonly as big as a Grain of Hempfeed, and ufually break out in the Face and Neck. Young People of both Sexes, when they come to Years of Maturity, are more fubject to this Diforder than others. Thefe Pimples are very red, and difficult to be cured; and though they vanifh at laft, the red Colour will remain for a long time. Thofe Remedies into whofe Compofition Camphire enters, the Effence of Benjamin, or the Sugar of Lead, are very efficacious in this flight Diforder. I am afraid that all thefe Hiftories and Particularities will tire you; for there are many things belonging to Arts and Sciences that pleafe thofe who profefs them, but are no way amufing to fuch as do not make them their only Study. If you pleafe I will here finifh my Medical Lecture, for perhaps your Ears begin to grow weary.

No, no, *Abdeker*, replied *Fatima*, I am not tired in liftening to what you fay. You have certainly made other Obfervations during the two Days you were abfent. You muft tell me all, otherwife I will not pardon you.

I was going to fpeak to you of fome Kinds of ruddy Spots, upon which I was confulted. The firft

Kind

Kind is that which Children bring into the World
along with them. Thefe Spots are more or lefs
large, and more or lefs brown. They are call'd
Moles. The fecond Kind is very common. They
are occafion'd by being expofed to the Sun, when
the Skin is fine and the Complexion delicate. This
Kind is commonly call'd *Freckles*. The third Kind
happens to Women that are with Child, who have
the Skin cover'd with large tawny Spots or Patches,
chiefly on the Forehead. The fourth Kind is contracted by Age, and we often fee both Sides of the
Face garnifh'd with thefe Spots, and fometimes the
Forehead, the Cheeks, and the Chin fhare the fame
Fate. There are fome Spots which are worth preferving; thofe, for example, that give a certain Grace
to the Face, fet off the Whitenefs of the Skin, and
give the Eye a fine amorous Look. In this Cafe
one fhould rather confult the Looking-glafs than the
Doctor; but one fhould not fpare thofe that are ill-
placed, efpecially when their Number is apt to hide
the Features that are moft capable of charming or
attracting the Spectator's Eye. Such Freckles as
thefe can hardly be taken away without Cauftics;
but we fhould never ufe any in fuch Cafes but the
milder Sort. It is alfo neceffary to take the utmoft
Precautions in their Adminiftration; for otherwife
they may leave a Scar behind them, which will occafion a greater Deformity than the Freckles themfelves. The beft Remedies in thefe Cafes are the
diftill'd Water of the great Scrophularia, which is a
mild Cauftic; or the Oil of Tartar *per Deliquium*,
which is ftronger, and may be render'd more mild
by

by mixing it with Rofe-Water or Plantain-Water.
One may ufe alfo, but with lefs Succefs, the Water
that is drawn from the Flowers of Beans and Elder;
which Flowers may likewife be boil'd in Milk, together with the Crum of White Bread. Thofe Remedies may be ufeful in all thefe Cafes.

As to what regards the Remedies that are to be
prefcribed againft the Effects of Sun-burn or Freckles,
you may ufe the Oils of Ben, of Eggs, of fweet
Almonds, and of the four Cold Seeds. One may
alfo order Afs's Milk, Breaft-Milk, Almond Emul-
fions, Pomatum into whofe Compofition the Butter
of Cacao enters; as alfo *Sperma Ceti*, and the Bal-
fam of *Mecca*. Some Women ufe no other Remedy
but the Yolk of an Egg beaten in Oil of Flower-de-
Luce. Others apply a yellow Cloth, which they
prepare with the Yolks of Eggs and *Sperma Ceti*. *

I REMEMBER, fays *Fatima*, that it was with the
like Remedies you fucceeded in the Cafe of *Zinzima*. I interrupt you only to let you know that I
forget nothing of what you tell me.

THE third Kind of Spots, of which I have fpoken
to you, continued *Abdeker*, difappear after Child-
birth; therefore they require no Remedies, unlefs
one has a mind to employ thofe of which I made
mention above. In fine, the fourth Kind is like
boil'd Leather, and is contracted by Age. The
Skin is fometimes too thick, which muft be taken
away. In order to fucceed therein, Emollients and
Anodynes are to be applied; afterwards the mild

---

* See OBSERVATION II.

Cauftics

Cauftics of which I have fpoken. If any one defires ftronger Cauftics, let the Face be wafh'd with
the diftill'd Water of the Gut of an Ox mix'd with
a fmall Quantity of Salt. By continuing this Application for fome time, the Skin will become thin-
ner and finer. *

How odd is the Conduct of Lovers! *Fatima*,
who reproach'd *Abdeker* for his Abfence, was the
firft that commended him for doing the Duty of his
Profeffion. She own'd that he ought not to neglect
it, both on account of the publick Good, and the
great Benefit that fhe was defirous of receiving from
it in their Converfations. But do not, fays fhe, neglect to beftow fome Moments on *Fatima*, that fhe
may enjoy your Prefence which is fo dear to her,
and improve her Mind by your entertaining Lectures.
Abdeker inwardly applauded himfelf, becaufe the
young Odalike was fo well pleafed with his Excufe,
without any Sufpicion of the true Caufe of his Abfence. His Countenance became more ferene, and
Fatima attributed this Change to the Satisfaction
that he found in her Company. Do not folicit me,
fays *Abdeker* retiring, do not folicit me to come to
you; for Sympathy has fo united my Soul with yours,
that I can enjoy no real Happinefs but when I fee
and hear you.

* See Observation III.

CHAP.

CHAP. III.

Of a Plot against MAHOMET.

MAHOMET, at his Return, pass'd the Time in the Company of *Fatima*. He accounted those Moments the happiest in all his Life: But how cruel and unhappy did they seem to *Abdeker*, who, at the very Instant he conceived Hopes of obtaining his Wishes, became jealous of the Grand Signior for the Enjoyment of the sweet Object of his Desires! The young Odalike would fain have got rid of the Importunities of the Sultan, which became every Day more urgent; but perceiving no Means whereby she could escape them, she was obliged to depend upon Chance to supply her with some Resource or Scheme, which all her Prudence and Sagacity could not furnish her with. But is it possible to live long in Tranquillity upon the Throne? It can no more be expected than a perpetual Calm through the vast Extent of the Seas. *Mahomet*, who charged *Mustapha* and *Ballabanus* with the Command of his Army in *Albania*, was inform'd that the Plague reign'd in his Camp; and that this contagious Disease, which every Day made a fatal Progress, had already destroy'd the greatest Part of his Troops. This Piece of News was succeeded by another, which was equally bad. He received a Letter which informed him, that *Ballabanus*, fearing this formidable Scourge would carry off the rest of his Forces, before he could perform any Action that
would

would either redound to his own Honour or that of the Emperor, put himself at the Head of the Remainder of the dying Soldiers, animated the few Sparks of Courage that sustain'd their drooping Carcasses, and forced his Way through the midst of Fire and Sword to the very Walls of *Croye*; where he received a Wound, as he fought most furiously, which ended his Days. The News of his Death struck the whole Army with such a Panic and Disorder, that they retired to the Plains of *Tyranna*, which is within eight Miles of *Croye*. *Muſtapha*, fearing he should be over-power'd in his Retreat by so formidable an Enemy, made submiſſive Propoſals to *Scanderbeg*, who accepted them.

MAHOMET never loſt Courage by bad Succeſs: He knew very well the Inconſtancy of Fortune; he knew alſo how much it depended upon Skill, Patience, and Policy to fix it. He reſolved to make another Campaign in *Albania*, in order to repair his late Loſs with Advantage. As he was meditating upon this Projeɛt, *Muſtapha* arrived, and gave him the Hiſtory of all the Misfortunes that had happened ſince he abandon'd his Army. It is thus, ſays he, that the moſt neceſſary Members periſh, when the Body is deprived of its Head. Perhaps your Highneſs thinks that I came here to charge you for your Sloth or Weakneſs; or that, being excited by ſome diſſatisfied Members or Traytors, I came to breed Trouble or Diſquiet in your Mind. No, I ſwear to you by the great Prophet, it is your Glory and Intereſt that makes me ſpeak to you in ſuch Terms. I perceive that my Zeal is too audacious, but

but the Danger is great that hangs over you.———
What Mortal dares to raise his Voice in my Presence,
says *Mahomet*? Does he pretend to make me tremble? He is much mistaken; my Heart never knew
Fear. Speak, I hear you.——Your Troops, says
the Pacha, refuse to obey your Orders; the Number
of the disaffected Members increases every Day. The
Aga of the *Janissaries* has already taken up the Stan-
dard of Rebellion. Are these the Examples, cry
your insolent Soldiers, which his illustrious Predecessors have given the Sultan? Shall their Victories
become fruitless to the *Mussulman* Nation? Is that
the Hero who made a triumphant Entry into *Constantinople*, and who has distinguish'd himself in the
most dangerous Battles? We disown him to be our
Leader, since he is altogether buried in Effeminacy
and Pleasure. What is the Use of all his fantastic
Projects? They have vanish'd like so many Phantoms. *Mahomet* sleeps, loaden with the Chains of
Love. Happy will he be when he awakes, if he
does not find himself over-burden'd with the Chains
which the Christian Princes, the King of *Persia*, and
the Sultan of *Egypt* prepare for him. Can it be
imagined that one only Woman should be the Cause
of so many Calamities, and should be an Obstacle
to the victorious Troops of the Emperor? Let him
kneel, if he pleases, before his Idol; but the Ado-
rer and his Idol will perish together.

MAHOMET could scarce curb his Rage, and
looking furiously at *Mustapha* spoke in this Manner.
When was there ever an Instance, that he who was
born to give Laws received them from such as were
born

born to obey? I know all the Intrigues belonging to Confpiracies. Rebels commonly feek Pretences, and endeavour to render the Perfon whom they would deftroy as odious as they can: But I am a Match for them all; and I will give my People an Example that will aftonifh their Barbarity. O ungrateful Nation! I muft needs bear an Iron Scepter to govern you with, and you deferve to have none but a Tyrant to rule over you.

I KNOW, replied *Muftapha*, that a Sultan fhould not be obliged to fubmit to the Whims of his Subjeƈts. The Sacrifice that the Seditious require is a Crime that fhould be avoided. Keep ftill your Miftrefs; fhe may accompany you at the Head of your Army, and order her a Tent in your Camp, and your refpeƈtful Troops will not murmur to fee her fhare the Laurels with you, and accompany you in the Path that leads to Viƈtory and Triumph. It is in vain for you, replied the Sultan, to endeavour to calm my Grief, or to divert the Stroke that is prepared for me. I fhall punifh the Infolent, after juftifying my Courage before their Faces, and after fhewing them how much I am Mafter of my Paffions. Command all the Officers of my Troops to affemble forthwith before the Gate of our Palace. I pardon you your Boldnefs on account of our common Education, and the faithful Services you have render'd me. Be gone; execute my Orders.

MAHOMET underftood very well, that to appeafe fuch a Tumult it was neceffary to fhed fome Blood: But in what Blood fhould he imbrue his Hands? Could he find in his Heart to plunge a

Dagger

Dagger into the Breaſt of *Fatima?* No, no, ſaid he, let us ſtrike, but let it be a Stroke that will no way affect my Heart, and that will overwhelm with Grief this barbarous Nation.

CHAP. IV.

Of the Death of IRENE.

*M*AHOMET had already pitch'd upon his Victim. *Irene* was the Favourite he was to ſacrifice. He loved this young *Grecian* Lady beyond Imagination, and ſhe was alſo the deareſt Friend that *Fatima* had in the Seraglio. *Fatima*, though become her Rival, never made the leaſt Step to ſupplant her in her Conqueſt. On the contrary, *Irene* had remark'd, ſince the private Conference ſhe had with her, that ſhe received the Sultan ſo coldly, that he was obliged to come back to his former Miſtreſs; who was well pleaſed to ſee that the Emperor ſolicited in vain to quench his Flame at the Feet of the inexorable *Fatima*. One might ſay that it was rather an Inſult on the young *Grecian* Lady, than a Proof of the Conſtancy of *Mahomet*, and that it ſhew'd the Aſcendant and Superiority of the Charms of *Fatima*.

IRENE was fair, which is not very common with the *Grecian* Beauties. She was ſtill in the firſt Flower of her Youth, and in all the Eaſt never was born ſo charming a Creature. A Pacha made her

N a Slave

a Slave at the Taking of *Conſtantinople*, and beſtow'd her on the Sultan, whoſe Heart immediately felt what deep Impreſſion ſuch agreeable Features are able to make. The Charms of *Fatima*, that were as great as thoſe of *Irene*, and more ſeducing, were only able to free the Emperor from that domineering Paſſion. Nevertheleſs *Mahomet* always ſhew'd *Irene* all poſſible Marks of the Love and Eſteem that were due to a Perſon of her Beauty and Character. There was no one for whom he had more Complaiſance. *Irene* diſpoſed as ſhe thought proper of the moſt important Employments in the Empire, granted Pardons, and directed as ſhe pleaſed the Will of the Sultan. In a Word, under the Shade of the Seraglio ſhe govern'd in the Divan. The Emperor was always very intimate with her; and although in the Bottom of his Heart he gave at this Time the Preference to *Fatima*, nevertheleſs he miſs'd no Occaſion of gratifying *Irene*. The Regard that *Mahomet*, though her abſolute Maſter, had for her was ſo great, that he endeavour'd to diſguiſe the Love he had for any other Object. Would he have acted otherwiſe if he feared her? But his Conduct in that reſpect was only a neceſſary Conſequence of the great Eſteem he had for this beautiful *Grecian* Lady. Formerly, contrary to his Cuſtom, he truſted the entire Management of State-Affairs to his Vizirs, that he might not be interrupted in his Amours. Theſe People being now under Diſgrace had murmur'd highly againſt him, and had conceived an implacable Hatred for the very Name of *Irene*. This Hatred, although founded only upon Prejudice, entertain'd

and

and fomented by difaffected Members, was the Seed of Difcord, which demands nothing more than to favour its Growth.

AFTER *Muſtapha* was gone, *Mahomet* enter'd the Apartment of his Wives. *Fatima* was the firſt Object that preſented herſelf to his Eyes. O *Fatima* ſaid he, with an anxious Countenance, you are the Cauſe of expoſing my Heart to many cruel Torments! For, to preſerve the Lives of thoſe that are under his Power, *Mahomet* may loſe his own! *Fatima* was ſpeechleſs at theſe Words, and knew not what to anſwer. The great Agitation the Sultan was in put her out of Countenance. She foreſaw there would be great Troubles, but knew not upon whom the Weight of them would fall.

THE Emperor enquired for *Irene*, and order'd ſhe ſhould be ſent for: He ſaid he had an Affair of the greateſt Importance to communicate to her. *Irene*, advertiſed of the Emperor's Trouble, and being well acquainted with his Cruelty, arrived. She look'd pale and trembled, imagining ſhe was to receive the Decree of her Death. Her Conjecture was well founded, as will appear hereafter. Take heart, my dear *Irene*, ſays *Mahomet*, affecting an Air more calm and diſſembling his Deſign; this Day you are to take full Poſſeſſion of my Heart: Fear no more my Inconſtancy; I deſign to eſpouſe you to-morrow, and give you the moſt ſignal and convincing Proofs of my Love. Let *Fatima*, vanquiſhed and confuſed for having preſumed to ſhare the Victory with you, be gone, and hide her glimmering Charms in the remoteſt Part of my Seraglio. *Fatima* got up with-

out

out making any Reply, drew down her Veil, and
went directly to her most private Apartment, to reflect upon the capricious Humour of the Emperor,
who without any manner of Pretence obliged her to
retire out of his Presence, after making her the
greatest Protestations of Love. This Way of acting
appear'd to her a mysterious Riddle.

MAHOMET staid all alone with *Irene*, and
paid her a thousand Compliments. In fine, says he
to her, your constant Love will soon have its due
Recompense. My Subjects shall know the great
Influence you have over me, and how much they
are to fear the Power of a Master who knows how
to pay due Honours to your Charms. *Irene*, who
truly loved the Sultan notwithstanding his great Cruelty, dreaded no ill Usage from his Hands. Sultan,
said she, speaking in a free and plain Manner, which
shew'd the Candor and Sincerity of her Soul, I expect no other Recompense for my Love than the Constancy of your Heart. You desire I should be united
to you by the Bands of Wedlock: The Marriage
will honour me much more than I can pretend to,
but it can add nothing to the Warmth of my Affection.——But how comes it that *Mahomet* entertains me with such Language to-day, who this Instant burning with the Love of another, seem'd to
have forgot me in his Seraglio? Without doubt a
sudden Disgust has withdrawn him from the Arms of
Fatima; it is surely so——nay, it is not so; be it as
it will, I dive no farther into the Matter: It is most
pleasing and most glorious for me to return again to

whom

whom I love, and to be the entire Mistress of all the Transports of his Heart.

The most cruel and most hard-hearted Man, and the most blood-thirsty, would relent at such tender Expressions. *Mahomet*, more hard than the Diamond, remain'd inexorable, and did not in the least change his Resolution. He braves Remorse, and triumphs over his Passion in the midst of all that might increase it. What had not the *Ottoman* Empire to fear under such a Commander? He retired with an Air of Satisfaction, but in the Bottom of his Heart he paid dearly for this apparent Tranquillity. Put on, says he to *Irene*, (taking leave of her) put on to-morrow your richest Garments: Let your Head be adorn'd with Flowers and precious Stones; let your Breast exhale the most exquisite Odours of Amber and Spikenard. My Reason for desiring you to appear in so magnificent a Dress should not make you suspect that I think you have Need of any Ornaments to please the Eyes of those that will crowd to see you: It is because the Splendor and Magnificence of the Feast requires that every thing should be conformable to its Grandeur. Oh the cruel-hearted Man! He contrived that his Victim should be well adorn'd before she was led to the Altar.

The impatient Soldiers got up before the Dawn of the Day, and surrounded the Gates of the Seraglio. The Officers also waited with no less Ardor than the Soldiers, all whispering about the Prey that was to be exposed to their bloody Appetite. In a Word, *Mahomet* came out in an open Chariot, with *Irene* by his Side. She seem'd more beautiful than

Aurora when she declares the Return of the Spring, and more brilliant than the Star that appears at the Setting of the Sun.   The Soldiers, dazzled with so many Charms, repented of their Rashness; they raised their Hands aloft to the Heavens, and cried out that nothing was comparable to the Charms of *Irene:* They might read in her Eyes a lawful Excuse for the Weakness of their Master.

THE Sultan, deaf to the Acclamations and Cries of his People, on whom he look'd with a fierce and wild Countenance, order'd he should be convey'd to the *Hippodrome* *.   He was hardly arrived there, when he got up in a Fury: Lightning was in his Eyes, and Thunder in his Mouth.   Cruel and ungrateful Nation, said he, with whom Tenderness is a Crime, and Inhumanity a Virtue! Since when, I pray, has it been accounted a Dishonour to the Memory of our Ancestors, to love an adorable Object? Behold *Irene*; it is she that has so often defended you from the Weight of this Arm: Oh, she is worthy of the Chastisement which your savage Vows require! Now, rebellious Nation, swallow in deep Draughts the Blood which once spilt will draw upon you and your Children the Curse and Scourges of Heaven! How unaccountable does the Conduct of *Mahomet* seem! He destroys the Innocent, in order to punish the Guilty.——Immediately was heard a confused Noise, in the midst of which one might distinguish Voices which demanded Pardon for *Irene*, and for a blindfolded Nation, which out of Prejudice and Pre-

---

* It is now call'd *Atmeidan,* or the *Horse-Market.*

cipitation

cipitation required a Sacrifice, of whose Value they are entirely ignorant.—— It is thus I accept your Intreaties, it is thus I relent by your Repentance, answer'd *Mahomet* to the amazed Multitude! At that Instant he drew his Dagger, and cut off the Head of *Irene,* who waited for the fatal Stroke with a profound Silence. She dropp'd like a Flower that is cut down by the Edge of the Plough-share. That Moment a ghastly Horror suddenly seized the Heart of every *Turk* that was present. Was a Scene of this Kind necessary in order to give a Lesson of Docility to this barbarous People? Heaven seem'd to be more sensible than the Earth, though dyed with such beautiful Blood; for it opened its Bosom, and made their Ears ring with its Thunder. *Mahomet* was so impious as to believe that the Heavens approved of his Crime: He went back to his Palace through the midst of Hail, Thunder, and Lightning.

C H A P. V.

Of the Grief of FATIMA.

*A*BDEKER being informed of the terrible News, trembled on account of the Danger which threaten'd the Life of *Fatima.* He waited with Impatience for the Moment that the Sun was to return to enlighten the Hemisphere with his Rays. The Day had scarce begun to dawn when he ran to

the

the Seraglio. He found *Fatima* bathed in Tears;
for the Sultan, all befmear'd with the Blood of *Irene*, came in Perfon to inform her of the tragical End
of her unhappy Favourite; and declared to her at
the fame time, that fhe was the only one that fhould
fucceed her, and that fhe muft quickly think of complying to fatisfy his Defires. She cried out, Dear
Abdeker, the Moment fhe perceived him! I have
loft the moft loving of all my Friends! Cruel *Mahomet* would fain perfuade me that his Action had ma-
nifefted my Triumph: He has alfo the Affurance to
tell me, that the Head of *Irene* was a Trophy well
becoming the Love he had for me! O that my Hands
were arm'd with a Dagger; I would find Strength
enough to plunge it into the Heart of this Barbarian! Can that inhuman Monfter pretend to affure me
of the Conqueft of his Heart, after deftroying the
Perfon whom it loved moft dearly? Heaven and
Earth fhall perifh before I grant him thofe Favours,
which I have heretofore refufed him out of Indifference and Difdain, but which I refufe him at prefent out of Hatred and Revenge. There is no doubt
but he will take away my Life. Death is the moft
acceptable Prefent he can make me. I will no
longer breathe the infected Air of his Seraglio: I
will fee no more that Tyrant whom the offended
Heavens have fent to punifh the Wickednefs of the
Muffulmans: I will be no longer conftrained to fhew
Complaifance to a Monfter that cannot be fed otherwife than by Blood and Slaughter. Perhaps the cruel
Man, perceiving the Advantages I fhould receive by
Death, will be fo barbarous as to refufe me that Favour:

vour: Yet even in that Cafe I can brave his Power;
there are a thoufand Ways which lead to the Grave.

ABDEKER acknowledged that the Caufe of
her Grief was very juft, and that it might be accounted a Point of Inhumanity to endeavour to put
a ftop to her Tears; but he was afraid that fome
lively Tranfport would take away the Object that
was more dear to him than his Life. Calm, faid
he, calm that Grief, my deareft *Fatima:* Let us endeavour to fhun that Fury which Hell vomits forth;
let us rather reflect upon the Meafures we are to take
in order to make a happy Efcape. The beft Means
that one can take to be revenged of that furious Tyrant is to deprive him of a Beauty whereof he never was worthy.

ALAS! dear *Abdeker*, cried *Fatima*, fpeak no more
of Beauty! In this Place it is accounted a Crime,
fince it is rewarded as fuch. Would to God I was
born fo deformed that I never had attracted the Eyes
of Men! I would, to be fure, if it was fo, live in
Solitude, and bufy myfelf about Things that would
not hinder the Tranquillity of my Mind. I fhould
never have known, perhaps, that there exifted a
bloody Executioner upon the Eaftern Throne, who
took large Draughts of the Blood of his Miftreffes.
But how can we efcape from this Confinement? The
Gates of this Palace are well guarded.——Then
fhe ftood up in a Tranfport and faid, What have I
to fear in feeking to make my Efcape? If I am
ftopp'd and taken, I fhall be put to the Torture:
What does that fignify? There can be no greater
Torment than what I endure, and perhaps I fhall
only

only haften the Death which is allotted for me.
Stay, my dear *Fatima*, cried *Abdeker*, taking her in
his Arms, ftay; you do not apprehend you will deftroy me by giving yourfelf up fo indifcreetly to
Death, which is already too certain. Do you forget that I love you? What do I hear, cried *Fatima*?
Abdeker fays openly that he loves me. O perfidious
Man! The firft Mark of your Love muft therefore
be to reftore *Mahomet* to Life, and the laft to keep
me in Chains! The Doctor, trembling at thefe Reproaches, fetch'd a deep Sigh, his Face grew pale
and dejected, and a Flood of Tears gufh'd from his
Eyes. Do you weep, *Abdeker*, fays *Fatima*, do you
weep? Oh, your Sighs difarm me! Judge you of
my Love.

SCARCE had fhe finifh'd thofe Words, when fhe
fwooned away upon a Sofa that was near her. Her
Pulfe grew weak, fhe ceafed to breathe, a deadly
Palenefs feized her Cheeks, and her Limbs grew
ftiff. *Abdeker* now feared that the Fatal Deftiny had
cut the Thread of Life of his dear *Fatima:* He
took a Bottle out of his Pocket that contain'd fome
Spirituous Water, whofe Effects were furprizing; he
put it * to her Noftrils, poured it upon her Hands,
and rubb'd her Temples therewith. *Fatima* figh'd,
and pronounced with a dying Voice the Name of
Abdeker. *Fatima*, dear *Fatima*, replied the Doctor,
(keeping his Lips clofe to her Mouth) receive this
Part of my Soul. How glorious will it be for me
to enliven fo beautiful a Body!

* See OBSERVATION **IV.**

FATIMA

FATIMA quite open'd her Eyes to receive the Light, whose Impression she felt to be more feeble than usual; and her naked Breast began anew the alternate Motions of Respiration. Without thinking of the Disorder she was in, she look'd towards *Abdeker* very tenderly, as he kiss'd her Hands, and bathed them with his Tears. You restore me to Life, dear Doctor, said she: Alas, how sweet does it seem to me to receive it from your Hands! Immediately she embraced *Abdeker* with such Transport, that he never presumed before that Moment to expect any such Tenderness from her; and she repeated to him a thousand times, that he was the only Comfort she had in Life. When the Doctor observ'd that the Mind of the Sultaness came by degrees to its former Serenity, and that the Storm which distracted all her Senses was calm'd and dispersed, he took leave of her, after making many Protestations of Love, and assuring her that he would come back to her immediately. Take this as a Token of my Love, said he, presenting her the Bottle which contain'd the Spirituous Water that restored her to Life. *Fatima* received it with Joy, and ever after carried it about her.

CHAP.

CHAP. VI.

Of the Manner of comforting the Afflicted.

AS the Husbandman, who is flatter'd with the Hopes of a plentiful Vintage, when he sees his Vines all loaded with Grapes, trembles at the Sight of a Cloud that is charged with Hail and Thunder; so in like manner *Abdeker* fear'd that Grief would alter the Beauty of *Fatima*. He dreaded that the continual Presence of her Executioner, or the Image of an inevitable Punishment, would lead her with a slow Pace to the Grave. For this Reason he did not fail to fulfil his Word. He redoubled his Care; perhaps he should have used more Precaution: But Love is blind; he was not aware of the Precipice till he was just ready to fall headlong from it. One while he entertains the Sultaness with some Project of making their Escape; but there is none of them all without unsurmountable Obstacles. Another while he tells her, how the hot-headed Temper of *Mahomet*, exposing him so often to evident Dangers, might free her from the Insults of this Tyrant. All this was still founded upon Uncertainty; yet every thing the Doctor said was deliver'd in the most tender Expressions, which engaged *Fatima* in some measure to believe him. The Marks of his Love were well received, and he was already convinced of the Regard the Sultaness had for him. There is nothing so efficacious for rendering us tender-hearted as Affliction, on account of the Sentiments of Compassion

it

it infpires. How little foever a Heart is prejudiced
in favour of any Object, its Defeat is certain that
Moment; it thinks no more of making any Defence. It is like a Citadel that is attack'd within
and without; the Lover may be affured of his Victory.

ABDEKER, willing to fhew *Fatima* how much
he partook of her Grief, firft fqueezed her Hand,
afterwards kifs'd it, and foon after embraced her in
his Arms moft tenderly, and confolated her in the
moft effectual Manner; affuring her that he loved
her, that he fhould always love her, and that his
Affection for her was as neceffary as a Declivity for
conveying the Waters of a River to the Sea. You
are the Ocean, fays he, to which all my Defires
flow, and from whence I draw the Water of Life.
When *Abdeker* had entertain'd *Fatima* in this Manner for feveral Days, fhe forgot her former Grief,
and became entirely comforted.

C H A P. VII.

Of PAINT *and* PATCHES.

AFTER *Irene* had been offer'd as a Sacrifice to
publick Revenge, and after the injurious Re-
pulfe of *Fatima*, *Mahomet* thought little of the Allurements of his Seraglio. Beginning to fear the
Enemies which he feem'd to defpife, he penetrated
into *Albania* with all the Forces he could get toge-

ther, and commanded them in Person. *Scanderbeg* had now a Rival that was an equal Match. The rapid Progress and Conquests of the Emperor was the Subject of all Discourse at *Constantinople*. He was compared to a Lion roused from his Sleep by the Anguish of the most smarting Wound he could receive. Animated by his Courage he attack'd all that surrounded him, and bore down every thing that came in his Way: Whoever opposed him became the Victims of his Fury. Happy Time for *Fatima!* Now she was not teazed with the Importunities of a Tyrant whom she so much detested: She enjoy'd peaceably the Visits and Conversation of her Lover; and his Presence was so dear to her, that whenever he enter'd her Apartment, her Heart leap'd with Joy. This Satisfaction she perceived might easily be discern'd by her Countenance, as it was soon succeeded by a Blush. The Eunuchs, who, to please their Master, interpret all the Proceedings of his Favourites, and endeavour to dive into their most hidden Thoughts, might well guess the Cause of such Changes; and they might account it a great Piece of Merit to reveal it to the Sultan, who would most severely punish the Offender for an Action that shew'd such a Contempt of his Love, and was an outragious Insult upon his Imperial Power.

ABDEKER foresaw the Danger, and resolved to shut up all the Avenues that might lead to it. To this End he proposed to give *Fatima* a different Countenance from what she had naturally. As an ingenious Painter he form'd artificial Features, that might serve as a Covering or Sheath to the natural

Colours

Colours that shone upon the Face of the Sultaness.
Formerly he invented a Kind of Paint that could
hide from the most penetrating Eyes the tawny Colour of the young *Zinzima*. Calling to mind this
Success, he thought he might also give *Fatima*'s Face
a fix'd Colour, instead of that Paleness and Redness
which alternately succeeded each other, when she
was agitated by the Motion that necessarily accompanied her Passions. He therefore chose Vermilion
to give a lively Colour to the Roses which began to
grow pale upon so beautiful a Skin. It was under
this apparent Veil he imagined that the Passions
might have their Play without being perceived by
the *Argusses* who endeavour to read and interpret
what the Heart imprints upon the Face.

As soon as the Doctor enter'd the Seraglio, he
found the Sultaness before her Looking-glass. She
seem'd that Day to be dissatisfied with herself; she
had cast-down Eyes, her Cheeks were more pale
than usual, and her Face had a languishing Air. It
is to you I must have Recourse, says she to *Abdeker*,
to repair the Vivacity of this Face of mine, which
begins to fade by Passions, like that of *Zelide*. This
Day it is so changed, that it frightens me to look at
it. If to-morrow I find myself in the same Condition, I shall break that Glass, which afflicts me by
its too great Sincerity. Curb that Anger, says *Abdeker*; I foresaw this small Alteration of your Charms:
It should not make you uneasy, for they will spring
up again with the Tranquillity of your Heart. You
should fear less for the present, than for the Time to
come. Your Face perhaps may decide the Matter

against us: We must hide the Sentiments that would undoubtedly cause our Ruin. The Eyes of your Keepers read and interpret the Motions which Love excites in your Countenance with Darts of Fire; therefore let us cover that faithful Interpreter of your Thoughts and Sentiments. At those Words he pull'd out a small Box that contain'd Vermilion; he took a Pencil, dipp'd it therein, and dexterously painted the Cheeks of the Sultanefs. *Fatima* consulting her Looking-glass, I do not know myself, cried she: Heavens! What a Prodigy! My Cheeks are as red as *Tyrian* Purple, and as radiant as a Flame. My Face is like *Aurora* shunning the Embraces of old *Tithonus*, and running to throw herself into the Arms of *Cephalus*. I remember it was thus that *Belino* *, by the Emperor's Order, drew my Picture upon a Piece of Linen. His Portrait was so true and lively, that I believed he had communicated Part of of my Existence to his Cloth, or that by his Magic Art he had enliven'd another *Fatima*. Pardon me this Crime; you know that the Maxims of the *Alcoran* forbid the *Mussulmans* to make a Representation of living Things; and this was the first time that I saw this Portrait. *Mahomet* order'd this Picture to be put up in his Apartment just by his own: But alas! most sad and unhappy Remembrance! Every

---

* A *Venetian* Gentleman, the Brother of *John Belino*, who had so great a Reputation in the Court of *Louis* XI. King of *France*. There is to this Day in the King's Cabinet a Picture that was drawn by *Belino*, at the Time that he was admitted to the Seraglio of the Grand Signior. He died in the Year 1501.

innocent

innocent Action of this barbarous Emperor is always effaced by a bad one. You saw how he proved to me the Violence of his Love, by inhumanly sacrificing *Irene*. He gave no less Proof of his Cruelty by the Method he took to let *Belino* understand that he had great Knowledge and Capacity in the Art of imitating Nature by Colours. This famous Painter employ'd all his Skill in drawing a Picture which represented the Beheading of St. *John* the Baptist. He thought that such a Piece would be well received by the Emperor, and by the whole Nation in general, who very much adore this great Prophet. *Mahomet* examined it with Pleasure, and discover'd great Beauties therein. But to shew that he did not judge like a blind Admirer, and that his Criticism proceeded from Skill and Reason, he blamed the Painter for not having studied the Effect which Nature is wont to produce upon the like Occasion in the Sufferer's Flesh. Applauding himself inwardly for this judicious Censure, and for his discerning Faculty, he resolved by a most evident Demonstration to convince the ingenious Painter of his Ignorance. He accordingly sent for a Slave, and cut off the poor Wretch's Head with a Stroke of a Sabre, giving by this means to the Artist a Model that was capable of solving the Difficulty. But *Belino*, more terrified than instructed, watch'd for an Opportunity of quitting a Master that endeavour'd to teach him by such bloody Lessons. He left this dreadful Mansion before I could have the Happiness of being acquainted with him. I give you this dismal Narrative, that you may have a more compleat Idea of the Tyrant that

makes

makes us groan under his Yoke. —— Oh! replied
the Doctor, turn your Eyes from such sad Objects;
give Attention to nothing but to your Lover pro-
strated at your Feet: He swears he adores you, and
that his Passion renews every Day with greater Vigour.   Look at that handsome Face, says he, (presenting her a Looking-glass) behold, your beautiful
Features have not in the least changed during the
melancholy Relation you have given of the Sultan's
Cruelty, though your Mind has been agitated at the
same time after the most violent Manner.   By this
Proof I thoroughly perceive the Efficacy of my Invention; but nevertheless your Eyes alone may difcover all the Secrets of your Heart, unless by your
Prudence you can hinder them from speaking only
what you desire to be understood.   Some time or
other perhaps we shall find out the Art of silencing
those Interpreters of our Passions, or at least to make
them counterfeit different Emotions of the Mind
from those they should naturally express.

SCARCE had he utter'd these Words, when a Fly
placed herself upon the exterior Angle of *Fatima's*
Eye.   The Sultaness perceived it in her Looking-
glass: Behold, says she, dear *Abdeker*, this little Fly
admires your Work very nearly: I will not punish it
for its Boldness.   I think its Blackness sets off the
Lustre of the Vermilion you have applied to my
Face.   I remark something more, says the Doctor;
that Fly makes your Eye look more lively and amorous.   *Fatima* turn'd her Head to consider more attentively the Effect of which *Abdeker* had spoken;
but away flew the timorous Insect, and deprived *Fa-*

tima of the Obfervation fhe had a mind to make. You are at no Lofs, fays the Doctor; I have found an Expedient to repair that Misfortune: We can for the future make feveral Experiments, without fearing the Inconftancy of an unfteady Fly. He immediately took a Patch of black Taffety, which was cover'd with Gum *Arabic*, and cut it in the Form of a Lozenge, and applied it to the Spot where the Fly had been placed. *Fatima* obferv'd that it produced the Effect which *Abdeker* had mention'd. I will let that artificial Fly, fays he, remain where your dear Hand has placed it. Give me the Sciffars; I have a mind to fhew you my Skill and Addrefs. At the fame time fhe cut the Taffety in the Form of a Half-Moon, and applied it to her Temples. It is not, fays fhe, that I defire to carry the Enfign of this Empire; the Poffeffion of your Heart is dearer to me than all human Grandeur, which is commonly purchafed at the Lofs of the Freedom and Tranquillity of our Mind: But it is to fhew you that my Love will ftill increafe, that is, if it be capable of receiving any Addition. Whilft fhe fpoke thefe Words fhe cut out another Patch, which reprefented the Full Moon, and placed it in the midft of her Forehead, faying, As this nightly Luminary eclipfes the Sun, fo in like manner do you rule over my Soul, in fpite of all the Allurements of Grandeur whereby *Mahomet* endeavours to captivate my Eyes.

ABDEKER was overjoy'd to hear fuch flattering Expreffions: He contrived alfo in his Turn an allegorical Symbol, that fully expreffed all the Sentiments

timents of his Acknowledgment. He gave the Figure of a Star to a Patch of Taffety. Permit me, says he to *Fatima*, to fix this Star upon your Cheek, since you are in regard of me that Pole-Star which directs all my Inclinations. After these tender Expressions, and after making various Experiments upon Patches of all Sizes and Figures, *Fatima* observed that she should not apply too many of them, and that one or two were enough. Afterwards she establish'd as a general Rule, that none of them should ever be put into the small Dimples which the Poets have imagined to be the Habitations of *Love* and of the *Graces*. She contrived likewise to give them different Names, according to the different Characters they imprinted on the Face. She call'd the Patch that was at the exterior Angle of the Eye *Killing*, because it contributed to give a sharp and lively Look; and named that which was in the midst of her Forehead *Majestic*, because it gives a noble Air. That placed in the Fold that is form'd in the Skin by laughing she nam'd *Jovial*; that in the midst of the Check, *Gallant*; and that near the Lips *The Coquet*. This last is also known by the Name of *Prude*, and the *Gallant* by the Name of *Jiltish*. In a Word, each of them had a Name answerable to the Effect it produced.

THIS innocent Diversion amused *Fatima* so much, that she forgot that her Physician's long Visit might be interpreted to her Disadvantage. In effect it was very late when *Abdeker* retired, and the Night had already begun to cover the Heavens with a gloomy Mantle.

As the Doctor stepp'd out of the Apartment of the Sultaness, he heard *Bachi-Kapa-Ogliani* * murmur, and threaten that he would inform the Emperor of his Method of acting.

CHAP. VIII.

Of the TEETH, *of the* GUMS, *and of the* LIPS.

SOME time after *Abdeker* came back to the Seraglio with a more jovial Air than usual. He thought it was necessary to lull that *Cerberus* asleep, before he could get to the *Elysian* Fields. In passing into the Apartment of the Sultaness, he purposely dropp'd a Purse of Sequins. *Bachi-Kapa-Ogliani* took it up immediately, and presented it to the Doctor, who refused to take it, desiring this vile Wretch to accept of it in recompense of his good Services. No other Method could have gained this mean Soul, who would sell his Services to the highest Bidder. The avaricious Porter niggardly lock'd up his Treasure, which was presented to him as a Bit of Meat is thrown to a Dog, in order to prevent his giving his Master notice that an Enemy is in his House.

ABDEKER advanced to the Sultaness, and told her all that had pass'd. Money, says *Fatima*, is the most somniferous Dose you could have given

* Porter of the Apartment of the Concubines.

such

such an *Argus*. Your Liberality has made me safe; for you must not imagine that Courtesy, Compliments, Officiousness, or familiar Condescension, could ever gain the Favour of such a Brute. It would be in vain to employ the Help that a good Genius and liberal Education have furnish'd, to move or gain such Animals as have no Sentiments. In this Case one must flatter their favourite Passions, which are commonly Self-Interest and Avarice. If you had not satisfied the Covetousness of that Eunuch by presenting him the Sequins in so ingenious a Manner, he would infallibly have ruined us in the Emperor's Favour.

AFTER these Reflections the Doctor thus addres'd himself to *Fatima:* I have prepared myself to entertain you this Day about an essential Point of Beauty, of which we have not as yet spoken, and without which all the other Features of the Face would be of no Value. Oh. you laugh!——It is because I guess what you mean, replied *Fatima*; you are going to speak about the Teeth.——Yes, says *Abdeker*; give all your Attention to what I say, for I shall go on in a grave and Doctor-like Tone; thrice happy if it does not become the Tone of Weariness!

THE Production and Formation of the Teeth are the Work of Nature; their Cleanliness and Preservation depend upon the Care and Help of Art. One may, without any Loss or Danger, be ignorant of the Principles whereby Nature acts; but to neglect the Attention and Management that are required in the Administration of the Instruments which she ordains for certain Ends, is of very dangerous Consequence.

fequence.   It is thus that one runs the Hazard of a
bad Digeftion during Life, if one neglects the Care
of the Teeth; becaufe by dividing and grinding the
Food they begin and promote Digeftion.

HENCE it is manifeft that the Teeth are of very
great Importance to the Health of the Body. They
are alfo equally neceffary for the Formation of the
Voice, the Articulation of Words, the Harmony of
Difcourfe, and the Beauty of the Face.   Hence it
is, that when the Teeth are ill ranged, or are far
afunder from one another, the Air which comes from
the Lungs being ill modified forms only confufed and
inarticulate Sounds, which difpleafe the Ear.   By
their Fall Beauty lofes likewife one of its principal
Ornaments; for the Teeth fuftain the Cheeks and
the Lips, and hinder them from changing into deformed Cavities and Wrinkles, the Tokens of decrepit Old Age.

BEHOLD the Confufion and Conftraint of *Axema*;
fhe dares not open her Mouth, for fear of fhewing
the Defects from which fhe might have preferved
herfelf.   If fhe fpeaks the leaft Word, if fhe gives
the leaft Smile, one perceives immediately her ill-
furnifh'd Mouth, which makes her look thirty Years
older than fhe is: A juft Punifhment for her Neglect!   I do not fpeak to you here of the bad Effects
that are produced by fuch culpable Sloth; as a bad
Smell wherewith the Breath is tainted, the loathfome
Colour of the Teeth, and Rottennefs of the Gums.
The Idea alone of thefe Defects is naufeous and dif-
guftful; therefore Care fhould be taken to prevent
them, or at leaft to cure them when they exift.

I AM

I AM not forry, fays the Sultanefs, that you have made thefe Obfervations upon *Azema*. She is a Slanderer, who tears unmercifully the Reputation of her Neighbour, though her Mouth be fo ill furnifh'd. She had a mind the other Day to make me believe that *Chryfolite* was deeply in Love with her Phyfician, and that fhe was the ftrongeft Motive which engaged you to make fo frequent Vifits in the Seraglio. I contradicted her, but without giving her any Room to judge of what I had in the Bottom of my Heart. I was too much concern'd to think the contrary, and I revenged myfelf by fpeaking in your Defence. I am inclined to believe you, replied the toothlefs *Azema* in a malicious Tone; but *Chryfolite* has received frefh Vigour, her Mind is more gay, fhe makes no further Ufe of odd and extraordinary Aliment, her Complexion is more lively, in a Word, her Face has recover'd all its Graces: I can make no Difficulty to believe that all thefe are fo many Marks of a fatisfied Paffion.

I ASSURE you, dear *Abdeker*, I was quite difarm'd by fo ftrong an Argument, and that Moment I believed you culpable. I queftion'd *Azema* very earneftly about every thing that could give me any Light into the Matter; for one would rather chufe to be expofed to too ftrong a Light, than to remain always blind. If *Abdeker* was faithlefs, I fhould account him the vileft of all Wretches; but I would require the ftrongeft and moft convincing Proofs before I could believe him to be guilty. Neverthelefs, will you have me tell you the Truth? Since that very Moment black Poifon has flow'd within

my

my Veins; but your Love appears to be such, that I cannot without ocular Proofs fear any Rival.

THE Doctor, astonish'd at such Language, threw himself at the Feet of *Fatima*, and removed all those Suspicions, by assuring her they were ill founded. This Commotion of Jealousy, says he, is the strongest Mark you could give me of your Love: Nevertheless curb that Passion; for its Beginnings are bitter, its Continuation is uncertain, and its End fatal. It is the greatest Harm that a Person can do himself, and the greatest Injury he can do the Object he loves. In short, we ought always to suppose the Object of our Love to be the most accomplish'd; for without that Supposition, Love is ill placed: But to impute any Treachery to it, or even suspect it of any such thing, is the same as to accuse ourselves for being deceived in the Choice we have made. It is also the same thing as if we should accuse the Object of base Sentiments, and of the greatest Imperfections.

PARDON me, dear Doctor, replied the Sultaness, if I unfold to you the most hidden Secrets of my Soul, because I think you should always know its inward Recesses, and that if I should endeavour to conceal the least Thought from you, it must be accounted a Theft committed against your Confidence. According to my Way of thinking, you are the most perfect Man in the World, and the most worthy of my Love. This is only a malignant Vapour that has exhaled from the slandering *Azema*, but which your Presence and your Candour have entirely dispersed.

P   IT

IT is an Attempt, says *Abdeker*, that I never will forgive her. I have found out Means to repair the Breaches which Age and the Badness of the Constitution make in the Mouth; but *Axema* may be assured that I will not offer her those Remedies *. It is very pleasing to find such an Opportunity of revenging such an Injury. But let us resume the Thread of our Discourse, which that cross Episode has interrupted. The Diet which is convenient for preserving Health, is also good for preserving the Teeth. If Digestion be impaired, either by the Want of Mastication, or by the bad Choice of Food, or, in fine, by the bad Quality of the digestive Humours, there will result from thence a thick acrimonious Juice, which will corrupt the Gums, and rot all the Teeth. Those who are troubled with the Scurvy, and such as have inwardly any sickly Ferment, daily furnish us with manifest Examples of that Kind. The Teeth of those who make frequent Use of Sweet-meats, Preserves, and Sugar-Plums, are commonly bad, and of a disagreeable Colour. After eating these tempting Poisons, one should never miss washing the Mouth with warm Water, in order to take away by this Dissolvent whatever sticks to the Teeth or to the Gums. Without this Precaution one runs the Hazard of losing those Instruments which are so useful to Health, and of being tormented by the most acute Pains and Disorders. I shall take care to conceal this easy Precaution from *Axema*. It is the Duty of the pious Iman, as he

* See OBSERVATION V.

explains to her the mysterious Sense of the *Alcoran*, to forbid her to eat so many Sweet-meats, or to prescribe her some Preservative against the Bitterness which is hid under so much Sweetness.

THERE are several Precautions necessary to preserve the Teeth. One should take care not to eat or drink any thing that is too hot or too cold. The Vessels that bring Nourishment to those enamell'd little Bones are hurt by too much Heat or too much Cold; and the Nerves, to which they owe their Sensibility, are irritated. Prudence requires that one should not strain the Teeth too much, by biting Threads asunder, lifting Weights out of Ostentation, cracking Nuts, or breaking any such hard Bodies. Such straining Efforts shake, shiver, and loosen the Teeth, and sometimes entirely destroy them.

ONE should likewise take care to eat with both Sides of the Mouth. Those who are accustom'd to eat only on one Side, hazard the Loss of the Teeth on the opposite Side; because the Teeth that do not chew are more subject to be corroded by the Tartar; they are more loose in their Sockets, and more oppressed by the lengthening of the Gums, which are commonly swoln in such Cases with a thick caustic Humour.

ONE should take care not to use Tooth-pickers of any Kind of Metal, or Pins, or the Point of a Knife or Fork, to pick out the little Morsels that stick between the Teeth. The Hardness and Coldness of those Instruments do them a great deal of Hurt. Tooth-pickers of small Feathers are the best, not excepting even those that are of Gold or Silver. One

should

ſhould not rub them with ſmall Bruſhes or Bits of
Cloth; for thoſe Bodies, being too hard, deſtroy the
Gums and looſen the Teeth. The beſt Way is to
waſh the Mouth every Morning with warm Water,
and mix with it ſometimes a ſmall Quantity of Brandy, in order to cleanſe and ſtrengthen the Gums. I
do not diſlike the Cuſtom of thoſe who uſe fine
Spunges to rub off the ſlimy Matter which ſticks to
the Teeth in the Night-time: Such Practice has nothing in it that is hurtful. One might uſe for the
ſame Purpoſe a Tooth-picker cut half round: But I
know nothing more proper for rubbing the Teeth
than the Root of Marſh-mallows prepared according to the Method preſcribed in the Sixth Observation; for it whitens the Teeth, without hurting the
Gums. If the aforeſaid Precautions are not ſufficient to keep the Teeth in good Order, one muſt
have recourſe to the Powders, Opiates, and Liquors
whereof I ſhall hereafter give the Compoſition, as
well as that of the Lotions which ſtrengthen the
Gums and correct a bad Breath. *

THE Teeth have not a greater Enemy than the
Filth and the Tartar which ſtick to their Roots, as
they make them turn yellow, and diſpoſe them to
grow rotten. The Tartar has its Origin from the
ſmall Morſels of Food which ſtick between the
Teeth, where they rot by degrees, and form a Kind
of Mud, which grows dry by the Heat of the Mouth
and the continual Contact of the Air. The Salt
which is ſometimes furniſh'd by the Spittle, and the

* See Observation VII.

Exha-

Exhalations of heterogeneous Particles which come from the Stomach, may adhere to the Enamel of the Teeth, there harden, and produce the foregoing Effects. All these Accidents may be avoided, if the Precautions, whereof I spoke a while ago, are put in Practice. If the Tartar be too tough or viscous, one must have recourse to rough Powders, and sometimes to the File, in order to rub off that heterogeneous Body, which, if let alone, would infallibly destroy the Teeth. Sometimes for want of Care the Disorder it produces becomes inveterate, and the Patient is only made sensible thereof by the tormenting Pains he feels, when the Teeth are quite rotten and worn away. When the Disorder rises to such a Pitch, I know no better Remedy than to draw out the Teeth, if it be not possible to cauterize them, or fill up their Cavities with Lead. I conceive how difficult it is for a delicate Lady to surrender herself to a Hand arm'd with a burning Iron, which would necessarily make her suffer the most exquisite Pains. This is the last Remedy that should be employ'd; since a Physician, whose Heart is sensible, suffers in offering an Outrage to Beauty. What do I say? It is no Outrage; it is repulsing with open Force an Enemy which does Beauty the greatest Damage that can be imagined. Such Women as have any Regard to their Charms have no better Way of repairing that Neglect, which has been so fatal to their Teeth, than to take a Resolution of suffering those aching Witnesses of their Carelessness to be pull'd out. This Expedient will procure them a great many Advantages: It will stop all on a sudden the Pain

that

that would otherwise have continued, whilſt the
Cauſe exiſted. Thoſe ſhining Eyes, on which ſom-
niferous Poppies could produce no Effeƈt, and which
never cloſed unleſs when they were overwhelm'd with
Fatigue, recover their former Sprightlineſs, after a
few Nights quiet Repoſe. Thoſe Cheeks, whoſe
Roſes, ſo often bathed in Tears, wither'd moſt ſen-
ſibly, reſume their former Colour. This Operation
alſo prevents the Corruption from being communicated to the neighbouring Teeth, which otherwiſe
would ſhare the Fate of thoſe that were condemn'd
to quit their Places. The Matter that cauſes this
Diſorder, like the Plague, corrupts all that ſurrounds
it, and by degrees infeƈts and conſumes the whole
Row with its dangerous Poiſon. This Operation,
which is ſo much fear'd, has another Advantage: It
ſuppreſſes the bad Smell which is exhaled from the
Matter that is retain'd and corrupted in the Holes of
rotten Teeth, and it prevents the Produƈtion of that
tartarous Filth, which adheres in great Quantity to
the Teeth, whilſt one cannot eat on account of the
Pain. In fine, by drawing the Teeth one eradicates
a thouſand Diſorders which accompany the Caries,
ſuch as Abſceſſes, Defluxions, and many other Evils
which expel the *Graces*.

I ᴅᴏ not think, ſays *Fatima*, that one ſhould need
to have ſo many Motives to determine him to get a
Tooth drawn. I think the Hopes of being deliver'd
from ſo acute a Pain is a ſufficient Inducement to ſub-
mit to the Operation. Notwithſtanding, ſome may
be ſo weak, or their Nerves may be ſo ſenſible, that
they fear the very Shadow of any thing that is like
                                                    to

to occasion Pain. Such People must be prevail'd
upon by the Force of Reason, and the strongest Ar-
guments are those that flatter Self-Love and Vanity.

THESE Reflections are much to the Purpose, replied the Doctor; but give me leave to interrupt
them, that I may pursue with more Attention the
Subject of our present Discourse. In the mean time
I am sorry that I have obliged you to shut your
Mouth; for it contains the finest Pattern that can be
found of well-ranged Teeth, and of Gums perfectly
form'd by Nature. Charming *Fatima*, open that divine Mouth, that I may be able to give a full Account of all its Beauties: I never shall find so handsome a Model.——You laugh! I perceive that your
Gums are form'd like the Moon in its first Quarter;
they embrace the Roots of the Teeth, and keep
them firm in their Sockets. I see they are of a Vermilion Colour, which adds much Lustre and Brightness to the enamell'd Teeth which they surround.
This opposite Difference of Colours, join'd to the
Regularity of your Teeth, and to the Carnation Colour of your Lips, form a most agreeable Harmony.
Methinks I see that shining Gate which leads to the
Garden of the *Houries*.

I PITY the Condition of those who through Neglect, or after recovering from certain Disorders, have
their Gums soft and flabby, swoln with black and
blueish Blood, growing beyond their due Limits, and
cover'd over with malignant and stinking Ulcers.——
Oh, you tremble! Even the Idea of such a Sight is
sufficient to strike any one with Horror. Fear no-

thing,

thing, adorable Sultanefs; I fhall not place before
your Eyes all the frightful Symptoms that accompany fo many Evils: I fhall only tell you in a few
Words the Remedies that feem moft efficacious to
me in the like Circumftances. Sometimes a fmall
Quantity of Brandy mix'd with Water fufficiently
ftrengthens the Gums, when they are fo foft as to
bleed by the leaft Compreffion. In other Cafes a
fmall Quantity of *Florentine* Orris boiled in Red Wine
forms a convenient Gargarifm for difcharging the
Gums when they are fwoln by a ftinking and corrupted lymphatic Matter. In fine, the Leaves of
Scurvy-grafs are efficacious for freeing the Mouth
from all the Filth which is apt to infect it, for re-
eftablifhing the Gums, and for quelling the Caufe
of the Ailment that is fometimes diffufed through
the whole Mafs of Blood. In this Cafe it is the
Phyfician's Bufinefs to examine into the Nature of
the Diforder, and to attack it in its Intrenchments.

You fpeak, fays *Fatima*, like a Phyfician that is
not willing to lofe his Right; neverthelefs I have a
mind to interrupt you, and make my Learning fhine
in your Prefence. You have fpoke with much Judg-
ment of the Cleanlinefs of the internal Part of the
Mouth: I defign in my Turn to make a Differtation
upon the external Parts; and I require of you the
fame Attention that I have given to your foregoing
Difcourfes.

The Lips mark the Compafs of the Mouth, and
determine its Limits. That Ruby Colour which animates them denotes the Livelinefs of the Flefh. Their
Feeling, which is fo exquifite that the leaft Impreffion

fion is capable of tickling them, fhews that they are one of the chief Seats of Pleafure. It is for this Reafon that Love chofe them as a Manfion for its moft delicious Kiffes. Eloquence has pitch'd upon them to be her Throne; for what is more perfuading than a handfome Mouth? Did you ever hear *Pholoe* fing? Did not fhe convey to your Soul, by means of her Lips, Joy and Pleafure, together with all other Paffions?

I HAD already perceived all the Advantages of a handfome Mouth, when I beheld fuch as had large hanging Lips; or fuch as had flat Lips, which feem'd to extend a Mouth that was but too big already; or when I obferved others whofe Lips were cloven after fuch a Manner with fome cutting Inftrument, that they form'd a true Hare-Lip.

ALL thofe Objects excited a difagreeable Senfation in my Mind, which gave me Occafion to remark that the Lips are a moft effential Part of Beauty, and of confequence that fpecial Care fhould be taken of them. For this Reafon I attentively obferved every thing that can make them deform'd.

INTENSE Cold chaps the Lips, and fometimes cleaves them very deeply. All Kinds of Fat and Oil are efficacious Remedies for this Ailment. I obtain'd a Pomatum from a certain Perfon, which he kept as a Secret. This Compofition, though very fimple, is very emollient, and very proper for the Cafe I am fpeaking of. It is compofed of Goofe-Greafe and Pippins *. I have ufed it a long time with good Succefs.

* See OBSERVATION VIII.

THE

THE small Blisters and Pimples that come upon the Lips, in my Opinion, require no other Method of Cure than to be dried speedily, by applying thereto a Crust of burnt Bread whilst it is hot. By this simple Remedy the Lips soon get rid of those nasty Pimples, which are commonly got by drinking out of Vessels not well rinsed, or by drinking after Persons that have a strong Breath, or by touching the Lips with the Hands when they are dirty, or after they have touched Things that communicate their Contagion.

As for the Scabs which attack the Lips after some Fits of the Ague, it is the Physician's Business to prescribe the Remedies which are convenient in such a Circumstance.

AFTER *Fatima* had finish'd, *Abdeker* gave her high Encomiums, which she justly deserved for her great Skill and Understanding; and assured her that in Time to come he would confer with her about the most hard and difficult Questions in Philosophy and Medicine.

CHAP. IX.

Of the Discovery of IBRAHIM.

SOME pressing Business engaged the Doctor to withdraw sooner than usual. *Fatima* went down to the Gardens of the Seraglio, where she amused herself commonly with *Aglae* and *Nisaph*. These

two

two young Girls were attack'd with the Small-Pox
some Days before; and *Abdeker*, by his Prudence
and Skill, had master'd the most alarming Symptoms
of that terrible Distemper. The Sultaness, deprived
of her Company, endeavour'd to employ herself use-
fully in gathering Plants which enter'd into the
Composition of some aromatic Waters, whereof she
had a Receipt from her Lover. When she was at
a good Distance from the Palace, she heard Groans
and Complaints. An unexpected Cry made her at
first retire out of Fear; but moved with Compassion,
or led perhaps by Curiosity, she advanced, that she
might discover the unhappy Object, which was not
able to support its Grief. She approach'd, and saw
Ibrahim all cover'd with Tears, and prostrate under
a Bower to which the Rays of the Sun could have
no Access. He pronounced some Words, which
were interrupted by his Sighs and Groans. *Mary,*
says he, most tender Mother, in vain have you entrusted your Daughter to my Care! Most cruel Barbarians have forced her away from me, without taking away my Life!——You will certainly see her
no more; and perhaps her Ghost expects yours in
the gloomy Darkness of the Grave!

IBRAHIM was the Pacha whom the Emperor
employ'd to build the Temple which he dedicated
to his Amours, and to embellish *Eski Sarai* *, which

---

* Which signifies the *Old Habitation*. It is the Royal Seraglio, where all the Women that serv'd the Sultan's Predecessors
are kept. They never go abroad from hence, unless they are to
be married to some Pacha. These Apartments have Gardens

he appointed to be the Retirement of Despoine *Mary* his Mother-in-Law. This loyal Subject answer'd the Sultan's Expectations so well, that he received daily Marks of his Imperial Majesty's Confidence.

BUT *Ibrahim* did not seek Honour so much as Tranquillity; yet a most unhappy Accident had clouded the most serene of all his Days. He gave himself up entirely to Melancholy; nothing could comfort him, and he thought it a Crime to let one Moment pass without entertaining his Grief by deep Reflection. Solitude had something that charm'd him, and sooth'd his Grief by increasing it.

FATIMA could not approach the Pacha softly enough without being heard, and without making him quit that grievous Extasy, which obliged him, in spite of himself, to trust the Subject of his Sadness to the Echoes. *Ibrahim*, confused at his having been surprized in that Situation by the Sultanefs, thought to make his Escape. Stay, says *Fatima*, tell me the Subject of your Grief, and do not deprive me of the sweet Satisfaction of being useful and comfortable to the Afflicted.

THERE is nothing able to alleviate my Distress, answer'd the Pacha. It would be in vain for me to send forth useless Sighs and importunate Groans. Nevertheless, as you seem to be touch'd with my Affliction, and as my Heart is agitated by I know not what extraordinary Motion, I cannot, without doing the greatest Violence to my Mind, refuse to

and Pleasure-Houses for the Ladies to divert themselves; but there is no free Entrance, the Gates being guarded by the *Janissaries* and *Capigis.*

obey

obey you, and to difcover to you the whole Subject of my Difafters.——— But, great God! What am I going to do? fays *Ibrahim* in the utmoft Confternation. I am going to reveal Secrets of which all the World fhould be ignorant. You faw me weep, alas! What can you conclude from thence? Is it a Crime to have Feeling, to acknowledge it, and to fhew Marks thereof?

THE Sultanefs, unable to fpeak, imagined the Pacha was delirious. She could not help fetching fome Sighs in her Turn. You weep, adorable *Fatima*, fays *Ibrahim:* I am unworthy of your Regard. I now feel my Organs too much affected by the flow Poifon of Grief, which will foon give up my Soul into the Bofom of Peace. Bewail rather the Fate of *Mary*, who, in the midft of all her Grandeur, carries, unknown to any one, a Worm which preys continually upon her Vitals, and obliges her to mix her Bread with bitter Tears of Affliction. Alas! fays *Fatima*, What has happen'd to the tender Defpoine? fhe who by her motherly Care endeavour'd to cultivate my Heart with Virtue; fhe who by her Example has obliged me to embrace a Religion which is rejected in thefe Places. ——— But what do I fay? *Ibrahim*, you will betray me!

FEAR not, *Fatima*, replied the Pacha; I do not enquire into the Secrets of your Heart, nor am I capable of betraying them. I cannot give you a more convincing Proof of my Sincerity, than to difclofe to you what I had a mind to conceal. You will utterly ruin me, if you reveal what I am going to tell you. What fhould you fear after fuch Proteftations?

Q

teftations? —— *Mary*, Daughter of *George Bulcus*, Defpote of *Servia*, and Mother-in-Law to the Sultan, was *Amurat*'s fecond Wife. She had but one only Daughter by this Marriage. This Girl might be about your Age; and I had the fweet Confolation of feeing that the Precepts I gave her were reduced into Practice as fhe grew up. I did not know that Circumftance, interrupted the Sultanefs; I never heard that *Mary* had a Child by *Amurat*. The greateft Part of the *Turks*, faid the Pacha, are in your Cafe: I am the only one that was privy to the Delivery of the Defpoine. Give me leave to lay before you the principal Tranfactions which accompanied or follow'd the Birth of this Princefs. I am the only one that can inftruct you with relation to this Article.

AMURAT efpoufed *Mary* for no other Reafon, but that he might be intitled to poffefs his Father-in-Law's Dominions. Refolving by all means to ufurp them, he pluck'd out the Eyes of the two Sons of the Defpote; and alfo, by a more barbarous Action, render'd thofe two unhappy Princes incapable of getting any Children. By thefe tyrannical Means he deprived them of all Hopes of ever enjoying the lawful Succeffion of *George* their Father. The Defpote, in order to revenge thefe enormous and cruel Proceedings of his Father-in-Law, enter'd into that famous Alliance againft the *Ottoman* Empire, whereby it was agreed, that the Forces of the *Venetians* united to thofe of *John Palæologus* Emperor of the Eaft, to thofe of *Philip* Duke of *Burgundy*, and, in a Word, to thofe of all the Chriftian Princes, fhould reftore reſtore Liberty to the *Greeks*, and plunge the Half-Moon into eternal Darkneſs. But the Army of the Allies having loſt the Battle of *Varna*, *George* was obliged to retire back into *Servia*, and could have got no Conditions of Peace from the Sultan, if it had not been for the Mediation of *Mary* his Daughter. It was during the Time that this Negotiation was upon the Tapis, that the Queen was brought to Bed. As ſhe had juſt Reaſon to fear the Violence and Cruelty of her Spouſe, who had treated her Brothers ſo inhumanly, and who was reconciled to her dear Father only out of Policy, ſhe form'd a Scheme to ſecure her Daughter from the Dangers which threaten'd her Life.

As ſhe was born a Chriſtian, ſhe had a mind to bring up her Daughter in the ſame Religion; but it was quite impoſſible for her to execute her Reſolution. *Amurat*, very zealous for his Way of Worſhip, would be ſure to puniſh ſuch a Proceeding with the utmoſt Severity. Beſides, the Chriſtians who had perjured themſelves by violating the Truce of ten Years, and who had alſo engaged *George* to break his Oath, were become odious, and by her greatly ſuſpected.

This, however, was not the only Obſtacle, nor the hardeſt to be overcome: For one might ſuppoſe that this Child, after receiving from her Mother the firſt Elements of her Education, might ſtill preſerve in her Heart the Memory and Belief of the Articles of her Religion, and purchaſe Peace by her Silence and her Circumſpection. But her motherly Tenderneſs obliging her to open her Eyes, and to look for-

ward to the Time to come, she forefaw a thoufand
boisterous Storms ready to arife: For this Child
would probably hereafter give a Son-in-Law to *Amurat*; and this Son-in-Law would necessarily endeavour to make good the Pretensions of his Wife to
the Kingdom of *Servia*, and would undoubtedly
dispute it with *Mahomet*, who had already given manifest Tokens of his favage Humour, and who had
obtain'd that Legacy through the Injustice of his
Father. *Mary* could discover nothing but Danger,
wherever she turn'd her Eyes. On one Side she faw
two Princes who were equally refolved to maintain
their Right, and the Revolutions that were to happen in the Empire, which was torn in pieces by the
Armies that were employ'd in its Defence. On the
other hand she faw *Mahomet* thrusting a Dagger into
the Heart of his Sister by the Father's Side, and by
the fame Stab murdering his Stepmother.

Such were the frightful Ideas that troubled the
Queen's Mind: But yet she never loft that Spirit of
Constancy and Resolution which furnishes us with
feveral Resources in the midst of the greatest Calamities, and which enables us to parry the Evils that
without fuch Assistance would destroy us. *Mary*
acted like a Philofopher upon the Throne: She defpifed human Grandeur, and preferr'd the Pleafures
of a private Life to all the Splendor of a magnificent Court, where criminal Examples are much more
common than Virtue. Therefore she refolved to
chuse for her Daughter that Station of Life which
she would willingly embrace herfelf; and she took
the following Method to execute her Refolution. She
publish'd

publifh'd through the whole Palace, immediately after her Delivery, that the Child of which fhe was
brought to Bed was dead. The *Turks* took no great
Notice of fuch an Accident; for they were bufy at
this Time in defending their Lives and Fortunes
againft the Chriftian Powers of *Europe*, who had
confpired to deftroy them. All thofe that were entrufted with the Queen's Scheme kept the Secret very
faithfully. I was charged with the Education of
this Child, and to employ for that Purpofe whatever
Money the Defpoine could by any indirect Means
contrive to fend me.

THIS long time paft I have had an extreme Aver-
fion to living in the Court of fuch a hot-headed
Mafter as *Amurat*, and much more in that of his
cruel Son. I thought of nothing more than to procure myfelf fome Place of Retirement, which could
excite no Sufpicion in the Emperor's Mind, who is
always upon his Guard againft any Surprize. *Mary*
knew my Honefty, and my Zeal both for the Intereft of her Perfon and that of her Religion: She
therefore gave me full Liberty to act in that Refpect
according to my own Prudence and Difcretion. Under the Pretence of fome Infirmities which required
that I fhould lead an eafy Life, I obtain'd Permiffion
of the Sultan to retire to an Eftate I poffefs in *Mingrelia*. It was in this Retreat, wherein I fhould have
been fo well fecured againft the Tumult of the Court,
againft Arms, and againft Paffions, that I intended
to bring up the Child which the Queen had entrufted
to me, and which fhe parted from with as much
Regret as if fhe faw her defcend into the Grave:

Nor

Nor is it any Wonder, for she was the only Child
that ever she had.

AFTER the Queen had committed the Child to
my Care, I departed with a small Number of Servants, but all very faithful. I did not embark on
the *Euxine* Sea, for fear *Amurat* (who had order'd
that an exact Account should be given him of all
that was imported or exported that Way) should be
informed of my Proceedings. I therefore resolved
to make the whole Journey by Land.

WE set out from *Adrianople* * without being in
the least observ'd, and travell'd very fast till we got
to a certain Distance from that City. The scorching
Heat of the Sun obliged us to perform our Journey
by Night; by which means we avoided both a great
deal of Fatigue, and the curious Remarks of the
Inhabitants of the Cities through which we pass'd.
The tenth Night after our Departure we arrived in
a sandy Desert, where we could perceive no beaten
Road. The Night grew very dark, and there arose
a thick Fog; so that our Guides could only direct
their Steps by the Help of Flashes of Lightning,
which were very frequent, and increased the Darkness during the Intervals that were between them.
We heard all on a sudden a confused Noise, of a
great Number of Men talking one to another. They
surrounded us on all Sides before we could perceive
it. I received upon my Head a Stroke of a Sabre,
which laid me senseless upon the Ground; so that I

---

* This City was the Residence of the *Ottoman* Emperors before *Mahomet* took *Constantinople*.

could

could neither defend myself nor the Child, which
Mary had entrusted to me. Happy should I have
been, if I had been that Moment deprived of Life!
Then I should not be tormented this Day with such
bitter Grief and Anguish, when I think that the
Daughter of an Emperor, and of the most prudent
and virtuous of all Women, is a Prey and perhaps
a Slave to those Barbarians who are continually at
War with all they meet! At last the Day began to
dawn, and it was with much ado that I could open
my Eyes at the Approach of Light. I perceived
by my Side the mangled Carcasses of some of my
Servants, and saw the rest dressing the Wounds they
had received. They came to me immediately, neglecting their own Life, in order to relieve their Master, who abhorr'd his Existence, when he could not
see the Child that was committed to his Care. I enquired after the Child and her Nurse; but there was
none knew what was become of either. But alas!
I guess'd, to my great Grief, that I should never see
them more! That sad Idea made me drop down
senseless a second time. My Pains and Anguish were
so great that I lost all Sensation: However, by the
extraordinary Care of those that were about me I
was restored to Life, which ever since has been of
no Value to me: Nay, it has rather been a Burden,
on account of the bitter Grief with which my Heart
is fill'd. Some Drops of the Balsam of *Mecca* pour'd
into my Wound put me in a Condition to walk. I
was inform'd on the Road by one of my Guides,
that we had been attack'd in all Likelihood by those
Robbers who post themselves in certain Passages to

plunder

plunder the Caravans that go to *Perſia*. Wanting
Proviſions, and being all cover'd with Wounds, we
were obliged to ſtop at *Erzerum*. *Azor* was then
Kadileſquer of that City. Formerly we were ſtrict-
ly united in Friendſhip, and I might rely upon his
Goodneſs. I went to his Houſe, and gave him an
Account of my Adventure, but concealed from him
what related to the Child. Thoſe infamous Robbers, ſays I, were not content to take away my Bag-
gage; they alſo took away a Child which my Siſter
had truſted to me, in order to be brought up in my
Retirement. *Azor* immediately ſent for the Muſſe-
lin, and order'd him to ſend out Troops into the
Country, to ſeize upon all thoſe that ſhould be found
upon the Highway, who could not give a good Account of themſelves. I remain'd for ſome Days at
Azor's Houſe, that I might not only recover my
Health and that of my Servants, but alſo in Expectation of getting ſome Intelligence concerning the
Robbers who had taken away the Child. A great
Number of Rogues were ſeized, but no Information
could be got from any of them. I thank'd *Azor*
for his kind Reception, and prepared to take my
Leave of him.

I HAVE heard many ſpeak well of that *Azor*, ſays
the Sultaneſs, and am perſuaded that he miſs'd no
Opportunity of doing you all the Service in his
Power. That is very true, replied *Ibrahim*; for long
before my Departure he ſent People to ſearch both
far and near for the Child that had been taken from
me in the Deſert. He offer'd me Money to bear my
Expences, and ſent ſome Troops to conduct me as

far

far as *Mingrelia*. In short, I arrived at my Estate; and it was a considerable Time before I could find in my Heart to acquaint the Empress with the unfortunate Accident that had happened. I knew very well how deep a Wound it would make in her Breast: But at last I took a Resolution to give her a full Account of that tragical Affair. She answer'd me in the following Terms:

" Dear *Ibrahim*, our Eyes are too weak to pe-
" netrate the Secrets of Providence; perhaps I have
" sinned in attempting to sound its Depth. Alas!
" if my Tears were able to assuage its Wrath, or if
" it could be moved by sincere Repentance, I should
" see my Daughter again!"

Twenty Years are now elapsed since that unhappy Accident, and Heaven has not as yet been favourable to our Prayers. I employ'd all Sorts of Means to restore *Mary* the Object of her Wishes. I made a diligent Search all over *Mingrelia*, and in all the Country round about *Erzerum*, and order'd that all Children of her Age should be carefully examin'd, and any Child seized that could be found with two large Moles upon each of her Arms in the Form of a Star, which were the most evident Marks that the Queen observed upon her Child.

FATIMA grew pale at this Discourse, and being willing to conceal the Cause of her Trouble, she pretended to be sick, caused by standing for so long a Time. She threw herself upon a Tuft of Grass that was just by her. *Ibrahim* continued his Story, and finish'd with an Account of the Motives which engaged *Mahomet* to come to *Constantinople*.

IBRAHIM,

IBRAHIM, says the Sultaness, I own that the Cause of your Grief is very great; but Despair is the Mark of a weak Soul: Expect always that a Ray of Light will disperse that Cloud which you account impenetrable. In Circumstances even where all Hopes are taken away, a wise Man never desponds; he is always sufficient for himself, and never wants Means to satisfy his own Mind.

As soon as *Fatima* had spoke these Words, she return'd to her Apartment. *Ibrahim* conducted her thither, assuring her that the Weight of his Pain was alleviated by one Half, from the Moment she began to partake of his Grief.

CHAP. X.

Of the Anxiety of FATIMA.

FATIMA no sooner enter'd her Apartments, but she began to examine the Moles she had upon her Arms, and to which she never before gave but very small Attention. She made use of the Moments she was alone, and saw with extreme Surprize that their Figure was the same with those that *Ibrahim* had described. Upon this she cried out, These are the Stars which the Child of *Mary* should bear! How! Could I be the Daughter of that virtuous Spouse of *Amurat?* How! Is it possible? If it be so, I may expect to be regarded by *Mahomet* as his Sister, and may lay aside all Fear of being obliged

to

to satisfy the Transports of his Passion or his De-
bauchery. O Stars, which without doubt guided
me when I floated in a Sea that was full of Rocks
and Shelves, pour down upon me your favourable
Influence, now I seem to be just arrived in the
Harbour!

SHE threw herself upon a Sofa, where she pass'd
the Night in a violent Agitation, meditating upon
the proper Means to come at the Bottom of this
Mystery. Scarce had the Sun appeared above the
Horizon when she call'd *Chrysolite*, told her that a
frightful Dream had alarm'd her Soul, and that she
had a mind to see *Kara Isouf*, to give her an Account
of certain Circumstances of her Life. *Chrysolite*, full
of Zeal for her Mistress, and much concern'd to see
her so much troubled, immediately executed her Orders, and sent a Page to desire *Kara Isouf* to come
to the Seraglio. This was the Man that *Fatima* was
brought up with at *Cotatis*. Some Misfortune that
happen'd to him in his Affairs, together with extreme Poverty, had obliged him to sell this young
Girl, who made a Present of her to the Grand Signior. The Money which he got at this Time had
put him in a Condition of supporting the rest of his
Family, and of coming to *Constantinople*, where he
thought to carry on his Trade, and to receive some
Assistance from his Daughter (for he treated her as
such) in case she should gain the Emperor's Favour.
He was not deceived in his Expectations; for he enjoy'd all the Pleasure that could be had in an easy
Life, separate from the Tumult and Trouble which
attend those who are engaged in great Business.

KARA

KARA ISOUF arrived, and was introduced to the Sultaneſs, who received him with as much Affection and Submiſſion as if ſhe ſtill depended upon him. My dear *Iſouf*, ſays ſhe, you ſhould conceal nothing from me; anſwer ſincerely to what I am going to aſk: My Ruin or my Happineſs depends upon your Anſwer. Tell me frankly whether I am your Daughter. At this Queſtion *Iſouf* trembled, and for ſome Moments could make no Anſwer. Pardon me, continued *Fatima*, for having form'd ſome Doubts about my Birth; but if you knew how much it concerns my Honour and Happineſs to penetrate a Chaos which a well-founded Preſumption has form'd in my Heart, you would make no Difficulty to give me a direct Anſwer. I remember that whenever Family Troubles or Vexations darken'd your Humour, you uſed to ſay that you would treat me like an Orphan. Do not think that I intend to puniſh that Vivacity which a natural Conſtitution begets, and which Reaſon deſtroys. If I am your Daughter, I ought to reſpect you as my Father; if not, the Care you have taken of me during my Infancy, and during my Youth, ſtill obliges me to a greater Acknowledgment.

No, I am not your Father, anſwer'd the Old Man, falling upon his Knees before the Sultaneſs. That Confeſſion is not ſufficient, ſays *Fatima*; you muſt tell me what Parents gave me Birth, and how I came into your Hands. Alas! replied *Iſouf*, I cannot give you the leaſt Inſight into thoſe Particulars, becauſe I am quite ignorant of the Object of your Curioſity. In the dead Time of the Night, it happen'd happen'd that I heard a young Child scream at my Door. I rose from my Bed, and found the Infant wrapp'd up in fine Swaddling-Cloaths, and exposed to the cold Air and stormy Weather. I waked my Wife, and gave her in Charge this poor little Creature, that was so cruelly abandon'd. She warm'd you in her Bosom, (for it was you yourself, pretty *Fatima*) and gave you Part of the Food which was design'd for a young Boy, of whom she was lately deliver'd. This Boy died some Days after, and you became the Object of all our Tenderness. In the midst of our Want and Misery we thank'd the Heavens for having repair'd our Loss so well, by substituting a Child in the Place of our Son, whose angelical Countenance promised us good Fortune and Prosperity.

WHAT have you done with the Swaddling-Cloaths, says *Fatima?* I kept them as carefully as could be, replied *Isuf.* I presumed they might one Time or other serve as Witnesses to make the Child known to its Parents. No one ever came to claim it. You know very well, that the Neighbours always took you to be my real Daughter.——I desire you to send me those Cloaths immediately, replied the Sultaness. Come again to see me to-morrow, and let no one know what has pass'd between us.

CHAP.

C H A P. XI.

Of the SMALL-POX, of WARTS, and of CORNS.

THE Old Man withdrew, and *Fatima* began a-
fresh to employ her Mind in deep Reflections.
She was meditating upon the Inconstancy of Fortune
when *Abdeker* enter'd. She did not think it convenient to let him know that Moment the Cause of her
Trouble, but imagined it was better to wait for a
greater Certainty, that he might be the more surprized. How are *Aglae* and *Nisaph*, says *Fatima* in
an easy Tone? Will they escape the Claws of that
Monster which originally sprung from your Country, and will they be cover'd with Scars after the
Combat?

THERE is an Appearance that this Monster will
respect both the Life and Charms of *Nisaph* and
Aglae, replied the Doctor. You have Reason to reproach *Arabia* for giving Rise to such a terrible
Plague as the Small-Pox; but charge not the *Arabian*, who is the Slave of your Charms, with the
Iniquity of his Country. The Hand which has endow'd you with Beauty will defend it from the like
Insults; or will permit at least that those whom it
has invested with its Power may repulse and overcome that formidable Enemy?

Is that possible? says *Fatima*, lost in Reflection,
and giving no Attention to *Abdeker*'s Discourse.

I SEE

I SEE nothing therein that is impossible, answer'd the Doctor, especially when due Care is taken of the different Stations or Times of the Disorder, that is, the Times of its Commencement, of Eruption, of Maturity, and of its Declension. These different Stations are accompanied with different Symptoms, every one of which must be treated after a different Manner. After observing all these Circumstances, the Physician must change his Weapons as the Case varies; and by these Means he may gain a compleat Victory in a doubtful Conflict.

Is that possible? replied the Sultaness a second time. Just as a General of an Army, answer'd *Abdeker*, is much surer of obtaining the Victory when he knows the Situation of his Enemies, the Way they are to march, and the Measures they are to take; so in like manner the Physician, in order to be assured of his Victory, should be well inform'd of the Origin, Progress, and Termination of the Disorder. *

Is that possible? cried *Fatima* a third time. *Ibrahim*, I should believe it upon your Information; you had no Design to deceive me. *Jsouf*, I should depend upon your Relation; you are incapable of telling a Lie.

AT these Words *Abdeker* perceived that the Sultaness gave no Attention to his Discourse, and that she was intent upon something quite different from that whose Possibility he was endeavouring to demonstrate. What do you say, my dear *Fatima*, quoth

* See OBSERVATION IX.

the

the Doctor? What Torrent of Reflection hurries away your Mind? Do you forget that it is *Abdeker* who speaks to you? Can it be some new Calamity that is come to interrupt our Happiness? With this he threw himself at the Feet of the Sultaness, embraced them, and conjured her to let him know the Cause of her Trouble. *Fatima* recover'd from her Extasy, and made *Abdeker* sit down by her Side. Listen, says she, and try if you can comprehend the Decrees of the Destinies. I am the Daughter of *Mary* and *Amurat*; I can produce incontestable Marks which prove it. She then told him what had pass'd between herself and *Ibrahim*, and acquainted him of the ingenuous Confession of *Kara Isouf*. Behold these Stars! Do not they open me a free Passage to Honours, and should not they give me Hopes of enjoying a most splendid Fortune? I do not at all doubt but you are of an illustrious Race, replied the Doctor, transported with Joy and Admiration. Your sublime Genius and your noble Behaviour have long ago discover'd the Dignity of your Birth. I consider'd you as a Tree whose Head is handsome, and whose Fruit is delicious, and which mere Chance has produced in the midst of a Forest, whose Trees are all wild and barren. But, dear Princess, (for I shall no longer treat you as Sultaness) have not I Reason to fear, that when you ascend to the first Rank, you will not even look at your Slave? Your Happiness, which was so strictly united with mine, will then become the Beginning of my Misfortune. Fear nothing, dear *Abdeker*, answer'd *Fatima*; it is not my Way to prefer any one on account of his

good

good Fortune, but for the fake of real Merit. By
changing my Condition I will never change my
Heart; and *Abdeker* may be affured, that he will
have as much Command over me when *Mahomet* and
all his Court fhall acknowledge me to be the Daughter of *Amurat* and *Mary*, as he had when I thought
I had been the Daughter of *Ifouf*.

AT thofe Words the Doctor could not abftain
from dropping fome Tears, and threw himfelf a fecond time at the Feet of the Princefs. Get up, fays
Fatima, go and perform the Duty of your Profeffion: I fhall go and prepare every thing that may
better inftruct me in what I propofe. To-morrow
the Defpoine is to pay me a Vifit, and I expect that
Ibrahim will maintain in her Prefence the Truth of
what he told me.

ABDEKER took leave of the Princefs, and
found himfelf tranfported with fuch Raptures of
Love, that he pafs'd to the fecond Court of the Seraglio without perceiving where he was going. A
young Odalike, who follow'd him for fome Time,
afk'd his Advice about the Tetters which attack'd
her Face. - - - - - - - - - -

Here there was a great Chafm in the Manufcript.

- - - - - - - - - - - -
- - - - - - - - - - - - -
- - - - - - - - - - - -
- - - - - - - - a Diforder hard to be
cured - - - - - - - - - - -
- - - - - - - - - - - -

BEFORE he had done fpeaking to the Odalike,
Agathina came to fhew him her Hands, which were

all full of Warts. He advifed her to rub them often
with Purflane, and to cover her Hands with it in the
Night-time. He alfo recommended to her the Juices
of the Fig-tree, of Spurge, of Dandelion, of Ce-
landine, and of Wart-wort. In fine, if thefe Ex-
crefcences cannot be taken off by thofe Applications,
which long Experience has proved to be very efficacious in fuch Cafes, you muft have recourfe to Sal
Ammoniac diffolved in Water. This Remedy is infallible when it is employ'd with due Attention.
Make no Ufe of the Spirit of Nitre: It is true, it
takes away Warts, but it operates with much Pain,
and leaves behind it a difagreeable Scar. *

AGATHINA thank'd the Doctor for his good
Advice, and afk'd him at the fame time what Remedies fhe fhould ufe againft the Corns fhe had upon
her Feet, and which troubled her very much. If
your Corns are fuperficial, replied the Doctor, they
can be eafily pared away. If, on the contrary, they
have deep Root, there is great Precaution required,
for a Gangrene is to be feared. I could mention
a great Number of Perfons who haften'd their own
Death by endeavouring to walk with more Eafe and
Liberty. You fhould avoid all corrofive Remedies,
and be fatisfied with palliating the Diforder by diminifhing the Pain. You fhould wear foft and eafy
Shoes, and wafh your Feet with warm Water, wherein a fmall Quantity of Bran has been boiled, or the
Roots of Marfh-mallows; and keep your Feet in the
Decoction for two or three Hours: After that pare

* See OBSERVATION X.

the

the Surface of the Corns flightly. If you repeat
this Operation once every Month, you will find yourfelf much relieved.

THE beſt Topics that can be applied are the
Leaves of Ground-Ivy and thoſe of Houſe-leek:
You may alſo uſe the Leaves of Spurge. Galbanum is accounted very efficacious for taking away
the Pain; ſo is alſo Gum Ammoniac diſſolved in
Vinegar. I have employ'd with good Succeſs a
Pomatum compoſed of Bees-Wax, Hog's-Lard, and
blue Vitriol. *Abdeker* took leave of *Agathina*, and
withdrew immediately to his Apartment, where he
employ'd all his Thoughts in conſidering what might
be the future Event of a Diſcovery that was ſo ſtrange
at the Beginning.

CHAP. XII.

IBRAHIM *introduces* FATIMA *to her Mother* MARY.

FATIMA expected with Impatience the Return
of *Kara Iſouf.* Neither Ambition nor Vanity
had any Share in the Steps ſhe took in order to be
aſſured of her Birth and Condition: It was the Love
and Tenderneſs ſhe had for the Deſpoine *Mary*, that
obliged her to take all theſe Meaſures. She was
very much delighted in repreſenting to herſelf the
Joy and Extaſy which this tender Mother would feel
on the recovering a Daughter who ſhe thought had
                                                    periſh'd

perish'd most miserably. The Interest of her Amours
made her wish with no less Ardor for the Success of
her Expectation: For being the Daughter of *Mary*
and Sister to *Mahomet*, she could have no Reason to
fear that she should be obliged to satisfy the Passion
of that Tyrant, but should have the Liberty of re-
signing herself entirely into the Arms of her Lover.
The Day surpriz'd her in the midst of those agreeable
Ideas. She· was hardly out of her Bed when *Ijouf*
enter'd her Apartment, and presented her with the
Swaddling-Cloaths. *Fatima* sent a Page to desire
Ibrahim to come to see her; and as soon as he appear'd she cried, Dear, dear *Ibrahim*, I sent for you
to give you Intelligence about the Child whose Loss
you so much lamented. Do you know those Swaddling-Cloaths? *Ibrahim* was transported with Joy.
Yes, says he, I know them; they belong'd to the
Daughter of *Mary*.

HAPPY Mother, your Tears will now cease! Heaven has restored you your Daughter. I have no
farther Doubt about it, charming *Fatima*; you are
the august Princess whom we have so much regret-
ted! Make no Delay, says he, (throwing himself at
her Feet) to confirm your own Happiness and mine!
Let me see those precious Stars which the Daughter
of *Mary* should bear!

FATIMA uncover'd her Arms, and was urgent
with *Ibrahim* to conduct her immediately to the Despoine. We should reproach ourselves, says she, for
every Moment she passes in Grief, since it depends
on us to put a stop to it. *Ibrahim* applauded the
good Sentiments of *Fatima*; but at the same time he
told

told her how dangerous it was to furprize a tender Mother with this News all on a fudden. Moderate your Joy, fays he; I will go firft, and bring her into a proper Difpofition for feeing you. Accordingly he ran immediately to the Apartment of the Defpoine: He found her in fo weak and languifhing a Condition, that he trembled to fee the Danger which threaten'd the Life of a Perfon whom he lov'd fo dearly. He changed the Difcourfe, and made her Daughter the Subject of their Converfation; but *Mary* was fo deftitute of Hope, and fo prejudiced againft whatever could be faid to her upon that Head, that fhe look'd upon *Ibrahim*'s Difcourfe as a flattering Illufion: For which Reafon he was obliged to affure her, that what he told her was Fact, and that her Daughter lived; that fhe was in the Seraglio; that fhe was not ignorant of her Condition, and that fhe would have been actually in the Arms of her Mother, if he had not feared that fuch a fudden and unexpected Meeting would have caufed a Tranfport which might have been hurtful to her Health.

THIS tender Mother, as foon as fhe heard thefe Words, recover'd her Spirits, and would fain have ran to her Daughter; but *Ibrahim* hinder'd her, and promifed to fetch her. He went accordingly, and came back immediately with *Fatima*, who threw herfelf into the Arms of her Mother, loaded her with fond Careffes, and bedew'd her with Tears: She fhew'd her the Stars fhe had upon each of her Arms, and told her after what Manner fhe pafs'd her Youth; but the Defpoine's Soul was wing'd with

fuch

such extatic Joy, that she could give no Attention to what her Daughter said, but embraced her again and again.   At last she lost all Sensation; for being spent with Grief and Anguish for the Space of twenty Years, she could not bear the violent Transports of Joy wherewith she was seized the Moment she found her Daughter, whose Loss she had lamented during all that Time.

But what a dismal State was *Fatima* in, when she perceived that her Mother fainted away! The Fits which her Grief had occasioned lasted so long that her Life was in Danger.   *Abdeker* came immediately to her Assistance. By his Presence and Care he restored this Princess to Life, and his Love gave her great Consolation.

C H A P. XIII.

The C O N C L U S I O N.

MAHOMET was soon inform'd of the Birth and Descent of *Fatima*.   He raged like a Fury when he found that he was to respect as a Sister the Person whom he had devoted to his Pleasures; and what compleated his Rage were the Thoughts of having sacrificed *Irene*: Useless Sacrifice, from which he reap'd no Benefit, but the Shame of being deluded by his own Cruelty! His Love was changed immediately into Hatred.   The Hatred of Tyrants never fails to produce its desired Effect: He therefore

fore refolved to deſtroy the Princeſs, ſince he could
not enjoy her for his intended Purpoſe. Immediately he diſpatch'd from his Camp a faithful Slave, with
Orders to poiſon *Fatima*. The Slave did not fail to
execute his Commiſſion; and *Fatima* ſoon fell into
ſuch a Fit of Lethargy and deep Melancholy, that
her Life was in Danger, and even deſpair'd of.
How deep muſt be the Concern of *Abdeker*, when
he perceived the Cauſe of her Diſorder! He knew
he could cure her, and deliver her from the preſent
Danger; but he knew that *Mahomet* had a thouſand
Means to bring her again into the ſame miſerable
Condition. In this Extremity he took the moſt extraordinary and the moſt unheard-of Scheme that
could be imagined. He concealed from *Fatima* the
Cauſe of her Diſtemper, and the dangerous Situation
ſhe was in; only giving her to underſtand that her
Recovery was nearer than ſhe thought for, and that
perhaps the Moment was at hand which ſhould render them both happy, and unite them together for
ever. At the ſame time he gave out through all the
Seraglio, that *Fatima* was in great Danger of her
Life. He declared openly, that the Death of this
Princeſs was at hand, that her Diſeaſe was contagious, and that none ought to be allow'd to come
near her Apartment. The Evening following *Fatima* fell into one of her lethargic Fits, which render'd
her quite ſenſeleſs. The Phyſician cried out immediately that ſhe had expired; and pretending that
her Body emitted a putrid Smell, which might prove
dangerous to the Women of the Seraglio, he order'd

der'd it to be carried directly to the Mosque without any Pomp or Ceremony.

THE Day before *Abdeker* went to the Iman, and offer'd him a vast Sum of Money to have the Body of *Fatima*. At first the Iman made some Difficulty of complying with his Proposals; but the Doctor telling him that he would substitute the Body of a Slave instead of that of *Fatima*, and get it cover'd with the Dress of that Princess, the Iman was at last prevailed upon. The Doctor follow'd the Body of the Princess to the Mosque; and as soon as all the People were retired, he made a Change with the Iman according to their Agreement *. *Abdeker* car-

* *Mahomet*, in order to dazzle the *Turks*, and to shew them his Zeal for their Religion, order'd a Mosque to be built in the Place of the *Temple of the Apostles*, which is call'd at this Day *Aboul fetch Sultan* Mahumed *Degiami*, that is, *The Mosque of Sultan* Mahomet *the Father of Victories*. He chose this Mosque for his Burying-place; and his Tomb is in a Turbet, or a Kind of round Chapel, wherein his Turban and his Belt are exposed to View. The *Turks*, who knew neither the Origin nor the Fortune of *Fatima*, shew Travellers another Turbet, which is very dark, and assure them it contains the Body of a Princess descended from the Royal Race of *France*, who embark'd in order to espouse a Despote of *Servia*, was taken by the *Turkish* Privateers, and given as a Present to the Sultan, who loved her very tenderly, but never could obtain her Favours, nor prevail upon her to renounce the Christian Religion. It was for that Reason, say they, that the Architect left a mysterious Obscurity in the Chapel; for they believe that this Princess, dying in the Darkness of Christianity, did not deserve to have her Body more enlighten'd than her Soul: But the *Turks* know these Circumstances only by Tradition. It is certain that this Turbet was the Place where *Fatima*'s Body was laid, and which the *Mahometans*, not knowing the Cheat of the Iman, firmly believed to be the

ried

ried his dear *Fatima* to his Apartment, where he soon recover'd her from her Trance. How great must her Surprize be when she open'd her Eyes, to find herself in another Apartment! You are deliver'd, dear Princess, says *Abdeker*, paying her his Compliments; you need not fear any more the Fury of that Barbarian *Mahomet*; your Life is secured.—— Oh, if you knew! —— He stopp'd, unwilling to let *Fatima* know the dangerous Situation she was in. He only told her that he was inform'd there was an Attempt to take away her Life, and that he had enough to do to save her. He afterwards told her by what Means he had succeeded in that dangerous Enterprize. *Fatima* could not refrain from Tears; the Life of her Lover was in Danger, and the least Suspicion was sufficient to bring him to Destruction. *Abdeker* chear'd up her Heart, and told her that he had freighted a Tartane in the Name of one of his Friends, and that they would embark as soon as she was able to bear the Fatigue of the Voyage. The Care he took of *Fatima*'s Health, and the Remedies he order'd her to take were so efficacious, that she was able in a short Time to undertake the Voyage proposed.

It was then that *Abdeker* told her what great Danger she was in, and the Nature of the Disorder from which he had deliver'd her. At length they

Burying-place of a Princess that was much belov'd by *Mahomet*. The Particularities of the Life and Death of *Fatima* agree very well with their Relation; which clears up a Point of History that never could be decided without the Help of this Manuscript.

embark'd,

embark'd, and arrived happily in *Italy*; where, after renouncing the *Mahometan* Religion, their Marriage was solemnized, and where they enjoy'd all the Satisfaction and Pleasure which Beauty and Virtue join'd with Wit and Good-nature could afford.

The END *of the* SECOND PART.

Observation I.

An excellent Water against the Gutta Rosacea, *or red Pustules in the Face.*

TAKE of Roch-Alum in Powder, a Pound; the Juice of Purslane, Plantain, and Ver-juice, of each a Pint; the Yolks of twenty Eggs: Beat all together in a Mortar, and afterwards distil the Mass. This Water is good against all Sorts of Itching and Ebullition of the Blood.

THE Water of Nymphæa, if mix'd with a small Quantity of Camphire after being dissolved in Brandy, is also very good in the like Cases.

THE *Virgin's Waters,* which we have described in an OBSERVATION of the First Part, are also very efficacious in the same Circumstances.

GREAT Precautions must be used in employing the Sugar of Lead, which is commonly put into Pomatums that are order'd for Ring-worms, Tetters, and Inflammations of the Skin. This Remedy, it is true, effects a speedy Cure; but it is dangerous to drive back into the Blood an Humour which Nature has already separated from its Mass, in order to purify it. This Humour, when driven back into the Blood, produces a vast many Disorders, lodges in some of the Viscera whose Functions are absolutely necessary for Life, begets the greatest Maladies and

the

the hardeſt to be cured; for it is not eaſy to bring it
back to the Place from whence it was expell'd.
Therefore internal Remedies are not to be neglected
when Topics are employ'd. Without this Precaution both Health and Life are in Danger.

Water for the Pimples of the Face.

PUT what Quantity you pleaſe of Salt-petre into
a Nodule of fine Linen; let it macerate for ſome
time in clear Water, then waſh the Pimples with the
ſaid Water.

Water for the red Spots of the Face.

BOIL together what Quantity you pleaſe of Sharp-
pointed Dock and Pimpernel, and waſh the Spots
with the Decoction.

Another.

TAKE a Pound of Veal, ſix freſh Eggs, a Quartern of White-Wine Vinegar, and a Handful of
Silver-Weed. Diſtil all together in a Bath-Heat;
waſh your Face with the Liquor that will reſult from
this Diſtillation.

Another.

TAKE the Water of Plantain, with the Eſſence of
Brimſtone; mix them together, and apply it Morning and Evening to the Face.

Another.

TAKE the Crumb of white Bread, let it ſteep in
Goat's Milk; then take an Ounce of Lime and of
Egg.

Egg-fhells: Put all into an Alembic, and diftil over
a gentle Fire. There will refult from the Diftillation an excellent Water to take away the Spots of
the Skin, whether red or yellow, and very proper
for whitening the Face, and giving it a handfome
Luftre. Some diftil together Cow's Milk and white
Bread, and to the diftill'd Liquor they add a fmall
Quantity of Borax.

You may alfo ufe with Succefs the diftill'd Waters of Rofemary, of Plantain, Marfh-mallows, Mercurialis, Chervil, &c.

OBSERVATION II.

Of Freckles, Sun-burn, and Tan.

*Excellent Receipts for changing the tawny Colour of the
Face.*

TAKE half a Pint of Milk, with the Juice of
a Lemon and a Spoonful of Brandy; boil the
Whole, fkim it well, remove it from the Fire, and
keep it for Ufe. Some add white Sugar and Rock-
Alum.

I ALSO recommend to wafh the Face at Night with
Spring Water or Pimpernel Water.

ONE may likewife bruife fome Strawberries upon
the Face at going to Bed, and let them dry thereon
during the Night, and the next Morning wafh it
with Chervil Water. By this means the Skin becomes frefh and fair, and acquires a beautiful Luftre.

It

It is one of the best Methods that can be used in such Cases; and the Prescription is not to be found in any Book of Cosmetics.

A Receipt for preserving the Face from Sun-burn and Tan.

TAKE any Quantity you please of Ox's Gall, and for every Pound thereof take a Dram of Roch-Alum, half an Ounce of Sal Gem, an Ounce of Sugar-candy, two Drams of Borax, and one Dram of Camphire. Mix all together, and shake the Bottle for a Quarter of an Hour; afterwards let it settle, and repeat the same thing three or four times a Day during the Space of fifteen Days, that is, till the Gall becomes as clear and transparent as Water. Afterwards filter it through Cap-Paper, and keep the Liquor for Use. This Liquor is to be employ'd when one is exposed to the Sun, or goes into the Country; but the Face is to be wash'd at Night with common Water.

Water for the same Purpose.

STEEP a Pound of Lupines in fresh Water for three Days; then take them out of the Water, and boil them in a brazen Vessel in five Pints of fresh Water. Take the Pot off the Fire when the Lupines are boil'd; and when the Water grows thick, strain the Liquor with Expression, and keep it to wash your Face and Neck, whenever you are obliged to be exposed to the Sun.

SOME add to this Water a small Quantity of Goat's Gall, Roch-Alum, and the Juice of Lemons;

and

and affirm it to be an infallible Remedy againſt
Freckles, if the Face be waſh'd therewith at going
to Bed.

THE Oil of green Olives, with a ſmall Quantity
of Maſtich, produces the ſame Effect.

SOME Ladies uſe the following Preſcription. Take
Deer's Marrow, put it into a ſufficient Quantity of
Water with Wheat-Flour, and let them ſettle; then
take ſome Ounces of what ſubſides to the Bottom,
and mix it well with a ſufficient Quantity of the
Whites of Eggs. Plaiſter your Face with the ſaid
Paſte when you go to Bed at Night, and waſh your-
ſelf the next Morning with warm Water. This
Method is excellent to prevent Sun-burn.

Water to take away Pimples.

TAKE equal Quantities of Houſe-leek and Ce-
landine, diſtil them in a Sand-Heat, and waſh with
the diſtill'd Water.

Powder for taking away Freckles.

CALCINE Sheep's Shanks, and reduce them to
Powder. Infuſe the ſaid Powder for four and twenty
Hours in White Wine, and rub the Face with this
Infuſion.

Water to take away the Spots of the Face.

TAKE two Pounds of Baſtard Rhubarb and Melon-
Seed, ten Swallow's Eggs, half an Ounce of Nitre,
and two Ounces of white Tartar; diſtil all in a
Glaſs Alembic, and waſh your Face with the diſtill'd
Water.

Againſt

Againft Ephelides.

Use the diftill'd Waters of the Whites of Eggs, of the Flowers of Beans, of Nymphæa, of white Flower-de-Luce, of Melon-Seed, of the Root of Orris, of Knot-Grafs, of white Rofes, of Crumbs of white Bread. You may ufe any one of them in particular, or many of them mix'd together, by adding only the White of an Egg.

Againft the Effects of Sun-burn and Tan.

Rub your Face with the Mucilage of Linfeed, of the Seed of Pfyllium, of Gum Tragacanth, and the Juice of Purflane, which you are to mix with the White of an Egg.

To take away the Spots of the Face.

Take two Ounces of the Juice of Lemons, the fame Quantity of Rofe-Water, two Ounces of Silver fublimed, and as much Cerufe. Mix all together, apply it to your Face going to Bed at Night, and the Morning following rub it off with a little frefh Butter.

Water which produces the fame Effect, and which makes the Skin bright and handfome.

Take a Pigeon, gut it, then fill up its Body with Baftard Dittany; put it into an Alembic with a Pint of Milk, three Ounces of Cream, fix Ounces of the Oil of fweet Almonds, and diftil all together. Wafh your Face and Hands daily with this Water, and the Skin will remain white, supple, and free from any Spots.

Water that takes away Freckles and Marks that come upon the Face.

TAKE equal Quantities of wild Cucumbers and Daffodil, dry them in a Shade, and reduce them to Powder, which you muſt infuſe in ſtrong Brandy. Continue to waſh your Face therewith till it begins to itch, then you muſt waſh with freſh Water. Repeat the ſame Operation every Day till you are thoroughly cured, which will be effeded in a ſhort Time, becauſe this Water is ſomething cauſtic, and of conſequence will ſoon take away the Spots of the Face.

THE Princeſs *Livia Colonna* employ'd this Water with much Succeſs. She learn'd the Secret of preparing it from a *Neapolitan* Gentleman who had travell'd in *Turky*, and had undoubtedly got this Receipt from *Mahomet*'s Phyſician.

Another for the ſame Purpoſe.

TAKE a Handful of the Aſhes of green Wood, and boil it in a Pint of Spring Water till it is reduced to one Half; then pour the Water off clear, let it boil a little, and filter it through brown Paper.

ALL the lixivious Salts diſſolv'd in ſimple Water produce the ſame Effed.

Another that is very efficacious.

TAKE the Blood of a Buck Hare, dilute it in an equal Quantity of the Urine of the Perſon for whom

it

it is defign'd, and filter through a Piece of Linen.
Keep it in a convenient Veffel, and ufe it after the
following Manner.

IF you have a mind to get rid of your Freckles,
you muft ftay in your Chamber for three Days; and
when you go to Bed, wet them with a fmall Piece
of Linen dipp'd in the above Water, and take care
not to rub it off. The next Morning repeat the fame
Operation, and feveral times in the Day for three
Days together. The fourth Day you muft wafh with
Pimpernel Water, and may walk about your Bufinefs. You muft ufe the Pimpernel Water four or five
Days, during which Time the Freckles fall off like
fo many Scales, or like Meal-Duft, and the Skin
will remain white, fmooth, frefh and fair.

Observation III.

IT fometimes happens that the aforefaid Remedies
do not produce the defired Effects, and are ufed
with little Succefs for the greateft Part of the Time,
becaufe the Skin was not fufficiently moiften'd before
their Application. Some Women in fuch Cafes ufe
the corrofive Sublimate, which requires the utmoft
Precautions. I rather commend the Conduct of thofe
who make ufe of the Lees of Briony, of the Herb
Cuckow-Pint, or of Figwort. As thefe Plants are
a little cauftic, their Lees are to be diluted in Flower-
de-Luce Water or Rofe-Water.

WHEN

WHEN the like Deformity threatens a beautiful Skin, one may employ, with Hopes of Success, Strawberry-Water, the Queen of *Hungary's* Water, whereof a small Quantity is to be put into fresh Water, the Oil of Tartar *per Deliquium*, Virgin's Water, the Liquor of fix'd Nitre, the Oil of Acorns, Nut-Oil, Snail-Water, Frog's Spawn Water. All these Remedies cleanse the Skin, and oftentimes take away the Spots.

OBSERVATION IV.

AS many Persons do not know the Difference between Baum-Water and the Queen of *Hungary's* Water, and as both are much used by the Ladies, I shall here give an Account of them both, with the Manner of their Preparation.

IN the City of *Buda*, in the Kingdom of *Hungary*, there was found in a Book of Devotion belonging to her Serene Highness Donna *Isabella* the following Receipt, dated the 12th of *October* 1652, with this Account prefix'd.

" I Donna *Isabella*, Queen of *Hungary*, aged se-
" venty-two Years, and being very much indisposed,
" was cured by the following Receipt, which I had
" from a Hermit, whom I never saw before nor
" after * : By the Use of it I entirely recover'd my
" Strength. It may also be useful to others. The

* I can give good Proofs that the Queen of *Hungary* had this Receipt from a Faquir that serv'd in the Seraglio, and had read the Manuscript which I am translating.

" King

" King of *Poland* propofed to marry me; which I
" refufed for the Love of God, and the Angel from
" whom I obtain'd this Receipt.

" TAKE what Quantity you pleafe of the Flowers
" of Rofemary, put them into a Glafs Retort, and
" pour in as much Spirit of Wine as the Flowers
" can imbibe. Lute the Retort well, and let the
" Flowers marcérate for fix Days; then diftil in a
" Sand-Heat."

THE following Receipt for preparing Baum-Water
was found in the Year 1593 at the Foot of Mount
Catmel, in golden Letters, upon a white Marble.

TAKE of the Leaves of Baum when they are
green, four Ounces; of Lemon-Peel two Ounces;
Nutmeg and Coriander-Seed, of each one Ounce;
Cloves, Cinnamon, and *Bohemian* Angelica, of each
half an Ounce. After beating the Ingredients that
require it in a Mortar, macerate all together for the
Space of three Days in a Quart of rectified Spirit of
Wine, and a Pint of Simple Baum-Water. Diftil
according to Art in a Bath-Heat.

OBSERVATION V.

*The Manner of preparing Marfhmallow-Roots for the
Teeth.*

THE Roots of Marfhmallows are to be gathered in
Autumn. They are to be chofen ftrait and fmooth,
and dried in the Sun, or in fome Place where they
will receive a gentle Heat. Remove them from
thence when all the Humidity is exhaled, and rafp

off

off the outward Skin, that they may become more smooth, and that they may be easier penetrated by the following Composition.

Take of the best Oil of Olives four Pounds, and of Alkanet half a Pound; put both Ingredients into a Copper Veffel that is tinn'd, set it over a Charcoal Fire, and, to prevent the Oil from burning to, add a Glass of Water. Boil the whole for half a Quarter of an Hour, then remove the Pot from the Fire, and let it cool; and take out the Alkanet, which by that time will have given its Colour to the Oil. Add also rasped Saffafras, Cloves, Cinnamon, *Florentine* Orris, Cyperus, Coriander, Calamus Aromaticus, and yellow Sanders, of each an Ounce. All being bruised in a Marble Mortar, you must set the Veffel over a small Fire cover'd with Ashes for two or three Hours. Then you are to put in the Roots of Marsh mallows, stir them often, and set the Veffel every Day for the Space of two or three Hours over a slow Fire cover'd with Ashes. At the End of eight or ten Days take the Roots out of the Oil, and put other Roots in their Place, till all the Liquor is used; and when you take them from the Oil, rub them well with a Napkin.

To render them more red and more perfect, you may take four Ounces of Dragon's-Blood in Tears, and two Ounces of choice Gum Lac. Reduce all to Powder, then mix it with sixteen Ounces of Spirit of Wine rectified, or the Queen of *Hungary*'s Water, in a Matrafs that must be larger by one Half than is required to contain the Whole; which you must stop exactly, and place it in a Sand-Heat for

T

four

four and twenty Hours. Stir the Contents from time
to time; then remove it from the Fire, and rub the
Mixture on the Roots with your Fingers. By this
Preparation they will acquire the Colour of a handfome red Varnifh.

An Opiate for cleanfing the Teeth.

TAKE red Coral, and Dragon's-Blood in Tears,
of each an Ounce; of Seed-Pearl half an Ounce;
of Crabs-Eyes, *Armenian* Bole, Seal'd Earth, and
Blood-Stone, of each three Drams. The whole being reduced to fine Powder is to be incorporated
with a fufficient Quantity of Honey of Rofes to
make an Opiate of a foft Confiftence. This Mixture is to be put into a Veffel twice as large as is neceffary to contain the whole, on account of the Fer-
mentation of the Ingredients, during which the Mafs
is to be ftirr'd once or twice a Day with a wooden
Spatula. You may add, if you think proper, four
or five Drops of the Effence of Cinnamon, and as
much of that of Cloves, which will increafe both
the Smell and Virtue of the whole Compofition.

Another.

TAKE red Coral prepared, the inward Part of the
Cuttle-Fifh-Bone, Cream of Tartar, *Florentine* Orris, and Pumice-Stone, of each one Ounce; of Sal
Ammoniac a Dram. Reduce the whole to fine Powder, and incorporate it with the Syrup of Kermes
and Vermilion. For every Ounce of Syrup put
two Drops of the Effence of Cinnamon and Cloves.

Thofe

Those that love Perfumes may add a few Grains of Amber or Musk.

This Opiate is to be applied to the Gums at Night going to Bed.

Some use with good Success the Juice of Lemons, or the Oil of Tartar *per Deliquium*, for cleaning and whitening the Teeth.

Observation VI.

An Opiate for whitening the Teeth.

TAKE Gum Lac, Coral, Dragon's-Blood, *Japan* Earth, of each an Ounce; Cinnamon, Cloves, the Root of Pellitory of *Spain*, of each six Drams; red Sanders, Cuttle-Fish-Bone, Egg-Shells calcined, of each four Drams; of common Salt dried a Dram. The Whole is to be reduced to fine Powder, and mix'd in a Marble Mortar with a sufficient Quantity of the Honey of Roses.

Another.

TAKE Hartshorn prepared, Ivory prepared, Sheep-Shanks, Rose-Wood, Crust of Bread, of each an Ounce; all which must be burnt separately, and reduced to Cinders: Also Seal'd Earth, the Rind of Pomegranate, and Tartar of *Montpelier*, of each half an Ounce; of Cinnamon two Drams. The Whole being reduced to fine Powder and sifted, they must be incorporated with a sufficient Quantity of the Honey of Roses.

OBSER-

Observation VII.

A Powder for the Teeth.

TAKE the Powder of *Florentine* Orris, Cream of Tartar, and burnt Alum, of each an Ounce; Cloves, Nutmegs, Dragon's-Blood, red Coral prepared, of each half a Dram. Mix all together, and reduce them to fine Powder.

Another.

TAKE Coral, an Ounce; Dragon's-Blood, Honey burnt in a Crucible, of each four Drams; Seed-Pearl, and Cuttle-Fish-Bone, of each two Drams; Crabs-Eyes, *Armenian* Bole, Seal'd Earth, and Blood-stone, of each a Dram and a half; of Cinnamon one Dram; of Alum calcined half a Dram: Reduce the Whole to a fine Powder, and mix them together. Put a small Quantity of this Powder upon a fine Spunge, and rub the Teeth with it when it is necessary.

Another.

TAKE Sage and Flower of red Roses, of each two Pinches; of the Root of Orris half an Ounce; of the Wood of Guaiacum three Ounces; of the Wood of Rhodium a Dram; of Cuttle-Fish-Bone two Drams; of Mastich three Drams; Myrrh and Cinnamon, of each a Dram; Pumice-Stone prepared, and red Coral well pulveriz'd, of each six Drams; of red Sanders half an Ounce: Mix and reduce all to Powder. If you have a mind to make

an

an Opiate, you must add a small Quantity of Honey, or of the Syrup of red Roses.

Another.

TAKE red Coral, the Kernels of Dates, Pearls, Crabs-Claws calcined, Hartshorn burnt, of each one Dram; of Salt of Wormwood one Scruple: Pulverize the Whole. You may reduce it to an Opiate by the Confection of Alkermes.

Another.

TAKE Rose-Wood, burn it, put its Cinders or Ashes red-hot into Vinegar of Roses; let them macerate for twenty-four Hours, then dry it in the Sun, and reduce it to a Powder; with which rub your Teeth.

SOME use with Success a Crust of burnt Bread reduced to Powder, and mix'd with a small Quantity of common Salt.

A Liquor for cleansing the Teeth.

TAKE of the Juice of Lemons two Ounces; burnt Alum and common Salt, of each six Grains: Put all into an earthen Pan that is varnish'd, and let it boil for a Moment; afterwards remove it from the Fire, and strain it through a Linen-Cloth. Get a Bit of a Stick, and wrap a small Piece of Linen about one End of it, which you are to dip in the said Liquor, and rub it gently on your Teeth. Take care the Linen do not suck up too much of the Liquor, lest it should act with too much Violence upon the Gums and the other adjacent Parts. It is to be

used

uſed only once in the Space of two or three Months: If you would uſe it oftener, add one Quarter of common Water.

Another.

TAKE Roſe-Water, Syrup of Roſes, white Honey, Plantain-Water, of each half an Ounce; of the Spirit of Vitriol four Drams: Mix all together, and rub your Teeth with a clean Napkin, and then waſh your Mouth with Roſe-Water or Plantain-Water.

Another.

TAKE Sal Ammoniac, Sal Gem, of each four Ounces; of Roch-Alum two Ounces: After pulverizing them, put them into a Glaſs Alembic to diſtil the Water, which you muſt uſe after the ſame manner with the firſt Liquor.

Another.

TAKE an Ounce of Pellitory of *Spain*, half an Ounce of Alkanet, ſix Cloves; infuſe them in a Quart of Spirit of Wine, decant the Liquor, and let ſix or ſeven Drops of it be put into a Glaſs of Water, wherewith rinſe your Mouth.

Water for the Gums.

TAKE of the beſt Cinnamon one Ounce, of Cloves two Drams; of Lemon-Peel, and of red Roſes, half an Ounce; of Water half a Pint; of Scurvy-graſs four Ounces; of Spirit of Wine rectified ſix Ounces. Beat in a Mortar ſuch Ingredients as require it; digeſt

geſt the Whole for four and twenty Hours in a Glaſs
Matraſs, and afterwards diſtil in a Sand-Heat.

An Infuſion for the ſame Uſe.

TAKE of Cinnamon in Powder two Drams, of
Cloves half a Dram, of Roch-Alum four Drams;
pour on them a Pint and a half of boiling Water.
When this Water is cold, add ſix Ounces of Plantain-Water, of the Water of Flowers of Oranges
four Drams, of the Eſſence of Lemons two Drams,
of Spirit of Wine ſix Ounces; digeſt the Whole for
four and twenty Hours, filter the Liquor, and keep
it for Uſe.

Another.

TAKE Mace, Cinnamon, Cloves, the Root of
Pellitory of *Spain*, and Seal'd Earth, of each half an
Ounce: Bruiſe all together, and macerate during a
Month in a Quart of Spirit of Wine; ſtrain the Li-
quor, and add eight Ounces of the Spirit of Scurvy-
graſs. Put ſix or ſeven Drops of this Liquor into a
Glaſs of Spring-Water, and rinſe your Mouth there-
with. After that you may rub the Gums with the
Conſerve of Roſes mix'd with five or ſix Drops of
the Spirit of Vitriol.

A Lotion for ſtrengthening the Gums, and for correcting a ſtinking Breath.

TAKE *Spaniſh* Wine, and the diſtill'd Water of
Briar-Leaves, of each a Pint; of Cinnamon half an
Ounce; Cloves, and the Peel of *Seville* Oranges, of
each two Drams; Gum Lac, and burnt Alum, of
each

each a Dram: Reduce all to fine Powder. Add two
Ounces of Virgin-Honey, and put all into a Glaſs
Bottle, which you muſt place over hot Aſhes; di-
geſt for four Days. The fifth Day you muſt paſs
the Liquor with ſtrong Expreſſion through a thick
Piece of Linen, and then preſerve the Liquor in a
Bottle well cork'd.

WHEN you want to ſtrengthen your Gums, take a
Spoonful of this Liquor, pour it into a Glaſs, and
uſe one Half of it to rinſe your Mouth. Keep it
for ſome Moments before you ſpit it out, and afterwards take the other Half, and keep in your Mouth
a longer or a ſhorter Time, according as your Gums
want to be ſtrengthen'd. You muſt rub them at the
ſame time with your Finger, and afterwards waſh
your Mouth with warm Water. You may repeat
the ſame Operation Morning and Evening whilſt it
is neceſſary.

To render this Liquor the more efficacious, add
to the Whole half a Pint of Cinnamon-Water diſtill'd with White Wine.

THE *Turks*, in order to render their Breath ſweet,
and to whiten the Teeth and ſtrengthen the Gums,
chew boil'd Turpentine, which they call *Sakkis*, and
which the *Perſians* call *Konderuum*. Thoſe that live
boyond the *Indies* chew it all Day long, and are ſo
accuſtom'd to it that they can hardly be without it
for any conſiderable Time. The Spirit of Guaiacum eaſes the Pains of the Teeth, and keeps them
firm in their Places. Some Drops of it are to be
put into common Water, and the Mouth is to be
waſh'd therewith.

Another

Another Lotion for the Teeth.

TAKE three Pints of Water, put it into a Stone Vessel, plunge an Iron red-hot into it three or four times successively: Put into this Water whilst it is hot, of bruised Cinnamon an Ounce; of burnt Alum six Drams; of Pomegranate-Rind in Powder one Ounce; of Virgin-Honey three Ounces; the distill'd Water of Myrtle, the distill'd Water of Briars, Rue-Water, Vulnerary Water, of each four Ounces; of Brandy half a Pint. Mix all together, cover the Vessel close, and let it infuse in the Heat of the Sun, or in a Place wherein there is a gentle Heat, for the Space of four and twenty Hours. The Infusion thus made, pass the Liquor through a Piece of thick Linen, or through a Straining-Bag: Add two Ounces of Scurvy-grass, preserve it in a Bottle well cork'd, and use it as the foregoing.

WE have said nothing concerning the Method that should be practised in filing the Teeth, nor relating to the Precautions that are to be used in chusing Files for that Purpose. Neither have we shew'd after what Method Lead is to be put into rotten Teeth, nor how they are cauteriz'd, drawn, or fasten'd when they are loose. All this is the Business of the Tooth-Drawer, and for that Reason does not belong to this Treatise.

I SHALL only speak a Word or two about the Method that is to be used in putting in artificial Teeth in the room of those that are lost by Disorders or Accidents. This Method is practised not
only

only when several Teeth are loft, but also when the whole Row is fallen out.

MEN's Teeth are ufed to make artificial Teeth; fo are alfo the Teeth of Sea-Horfes, of Oxen, of Horfes, of Mules, Ivory, &c. Some make them of the Shin-Bone of an Ox, after it is whiten'd.

THESE Teeth are to be proportion'd to the Cavity they are to fill, to the Height of the other Teeth, and to their Colour; then they are to be faften'd to the next Teeth, either with common Thread, or with Gold-Wire. Some famous Artifts have invented compleat Sets of Teeth with a Spring.

OBSERVATION VIII.

Pomatum for the Lips.

TAKE the Oil of Violets, the Juice of Marfh-mallows, of each an Ounce and a half; Goofe-Greafe, and the Marrow of a Calf, of each two Drams; of Gum Tragacanth a Dram and a half. Mix all together over the Fire.

IF the Chaps are deep, you may add a Dram of Litharge; or you may ufe the cooling Cerate of *Galen*, which is prepared after the following Manner: Take eight Ounces of the Oil of Rofes, an Ounce of white Wax; melt them in a Glafs Veffel, and ftir them with a wooden Spatula. Let the Mixture cool, and wafh it well with clear Water.

Red

Red Pomatum for the Lips.

TAKE an Ounce of white Wax and of an Ox's Marrow, three Ounces of white Pomatum, and melt all in a Bath-Heat. Add a Dram of Alkanet, and stir the Mass till it acquires a red Colour.

OTHERS chuse to use the Ointment of Roses, which is thus prepared:

TAKE Hog's Lard wash'd in Rose-Water, red Roses, and pale Roses; beat all in a Mortar, mix them together, and let them macerate for two Days. Then melt the Lard and strain it, and add the same Quantity of Roses as before. Let them macerate in the Fat for two Days, and afterwards let the Mass boil in a Bath-Heat. Strain it with Expression, and keep it for Use.

SOME are accustom'd to wash their Lips with pure Brandy, in order to make them look red.

For Chapp'd Lips.

TAKE Tutty and the Oil of Eggs well mix'd together, and rub the Lips therewith, after washing them with Barley-Water or Plantain-Water.

SOME People affirm there is nothing so good in such Cases as the Grease that comes out of the wooden Ladles that are used in Kitchens, when they are put before the Fire.

A CRUST of burnt Bread, especially that of brown Bread, if applied hot, is excellent for drying up the little Pimples or Bladders that come upon the Lips after drinking out of Cups that were

used

ufed by unclean Perfons, or fuch as had a ftinking Breath.

OBSERVATION IX.

Againft the Marks commonly left by the Small-Pox after Suppuration.

YOU are to order the Patient to take a Vomit before the Eruption, and keep his Body loofe by means of Clyfters. Both thefe Methods dimi- nifh confiderably the Quantity of Matter that would otherwife come to the Skin; and they likewife hin- der the Malignity and Corruption of the Humours in general. During the Time of the Eruption you may put fome Grains of Kermes into the Patient's Drink. This Medicine purges gently, and at the fame time gives Tenfion to the Fibres. By thefe Precautions the Small-Pox feldom becomes conflu- ent, and the Head is preferved from the Symptoms and unhappy Accidents that always accompany that dangerous Diftemper.

ONE may eafily comprehend that the Application of the aforefaid Remedies fhould be made by a fkil- ful Phyfician, who knows the Strength and Confti- tution of the Patient, the Nature of the Diforder, and the particular Cafes that are not fubject to the general Rule.

THE feventh Day, when the Suppuration begins, you may apply to the Pimples the following Snail-
Pomatum,

Pomatum, whose good Effects in such Cases have been often proved by Experience. Others use a Pomatum that is made of old Lard; others employ Plantain-Water with Saffron; others make use of Lentil-Pottage; others order the Oil of Sweet Almonds and *Sperma Ceti*. The twelfth Day you may purge, in order to avoid a new Suppuration, which sometimes happens, and to hasten the Exsiccation of the suppurated Pustules.

THE red Spots will soon vanish, if they are bathed with Wine and Butter mix'd together. Ass's Milk is excellent for the same Purpose, and hinders the Face from growing brown or yellow.

A Snail-Pomatum.

TAKE as many Snails as you please, and beat them in a Mortar with a sufficient Quantity of the Oil of Sweet Almonds: Strain by Expression, and add an Ounce of Virgin-Wax for every four Ounces of Oil. Wash the Whole in the Water of Frog's Spawn, and add a few Drops of the Essence of Lemons, in order to correct the bad Smell.

Another Pomatum.

TAKE half a Pound of fresh Butter well wash'd, and half a Pound of the Leaves of House-leek; beat the Leaves in a Mortar, and when they are well bruised add the Butter, and incorporate it with the other Ingredients as well as possible. Then put this Mixture over the Fire, and remove it from thence when it acquires the Consistence of an Ointment.

Another.

Another.

BOIL what Quantity you pleafe of Calf's Chal-
dron. Put the Greafe that comes to the Top into
Spring-Water, and ftir it well with a Stick; then
mix it with an equal Quantity of Plantain-Water.
Add a fmall Quantity of Saffron.

Pomatum for taking away Pock-holes.

TAKE of Rofe-colour'd Pomatum an Ounce, of
corrofive Sublimate a Dram; apply it to the Pock-
holes with a Partridge-Feather. The Dofe of the
corrofive Sublimate may be increafed according to
the Circumftances: But the Adminiftration of this
Remedy requires the utmoft Precaution, left it fhould
excite an Inflammation or an Eryfipelas.

Water for the fame Purpofe.

TAKE the Phlegm of diftill'd White-Wine Vinegar, wafh your Face therewith when you go to Bed
at Night, and the next Morning wafh with a Decoction of Bran and Marfh-mallows.

OBSERVATION X.

WARTS may be extirpated four Ways. 1. By
a Ligature. 2. By cutting. 3. By burning.
4. By withering or eating them away. But each of
thefe Ways has its Inconveniences. It is proper to
examine them one after another.

1. THE

1. The Ligature is not to be practifed unlefs the Wart has a fmall Bafe; in which Cafe you may take a Horfe-hair, a Needle-full of Silk or wax'd Thread, and tie it ftrongly to the Pedicle of the Wart. But what is the Confequence of this Operation? The Part that is bound withers and falls away; the Root remains, and fhoots forth anew.

2. When the Warts are cut, there are two Inconveniences that refult from the Operation. *Firft*, The Root remaining entire, there will grow a new Wart, perhaps greater than the firft. *Secondly*, There may happen an Inflammation, which may occafion an Ulcer.

3. They may be burnt. To fucceed in this Operation, you muft heat a Needle, and run it through the Bafe of the Wart. Some ufe a red-hot Iron, which they hold near the Wart by degrees, till they feel a lively Senfation of the Heat. Some take the Half of a Nut-fhell, wherein they make a Hole, which they adapt to the Wart; and in the hollow Part of the Shell they put Brimftone, and fet it on fire. All thefe Ways are efficacious; but, befides the Pain they occafion, they fometimes caufe an Inflammation, and Ulcers in the Skin.

4. They may be wither'd or confum'd by Efcharotics: But all fuch Remedies are dangerous, and require the utmoft Circumfpection and Prudence in their Adminiftration. It will be far more fafe and advantageous to make ufe of the Remedies prefcribed in the foregoing Treatife, than to truft to fuch pernicious Drugs. Befides, the Remedies we recommend are very efficacious, very eafily procured, and

produce

produce no bad Effect. I fhall here mention fome of them, that fuch as defire to be freed from this flight Inconvenience may have them at hand, without giving themfelves the Trouble to look for them.

THE Leaves of Marigolds, the Juices of Figwort and Savine, the Juice of green Figs, Salt beai in the Juice of Horfe-radifh, common Salt diffolved in Vinegar, and Snails, are all efficacious Remedies in the prefent Cafe; and fo is Agrimony infufed in Vinegar.

SOME get rid of their Warts by ufing no other Remedy but Patches cover'd with Diapalma.

F I N I S.